"My life is a mess, Kasey, and I don't need any more complications.

"Can we keep it simple? You're my assistant and temporary nanny—that's it."

Yeah, that was it, that was all it could be. It didn't matter that they had enough sexual chemistry to ignite the room, they needed to keep their distance. She respected Aaron's big brain—and, because she was still a woman, she also appreciated his very excellent body—but she was not prepared to jeopardize her job or allow her heart to hope.

Aaron was still looking at her, giving her that steely-eyed, hard-assed look that he frequently used when dealing with a complicated work issue. He was right. It was essential they didn't make this situation any more complicated than it needed to be.

So Kasey absolutely shouldn't kiss him.

* * *

The Nanny Proposal is part of Texas Cattleman's Club: The Impostor series—Will the scandal of the century lead to love for these rich ranchers?

Dear Reader,

I am so pleased and honored to be part of the wonderful Texas Cattleman's Club series.

After finding out that her best friend had an affair with her husband, Kasey Monroe knows she needs a change of scenery. After her divorce, she interviews to be Aaron Phillips's virtual assistant, but before she takes the job they have a hot one-night stand, agreeing that if she takes the job, their encounter will be forgotten.

Eight months later and Aaron needs Kasey's help. His brother, Jason, has gone missing and Aaron cannot understand why he hasn't contacted his daughter, Savannah. Aaron, because he is named as Savannah's guardian in Jason's will, takes custody of his niece but he has a massive business to run and he needs help. He turns to the one person he knows he can rely on, Kasey, and persuades her to help him care for Savannah on a temporary basis.

Aaron and Kasey shouldn't be in the same room together because they are as attracted to each other as before. Aaron can't afford to be distracted—he needs to find Jason—and Kasey has both her best friend and her ex trying to reestablish contact with her. This isn't the right time to fall in lust, and definitely not the right time to fall in love!

Happy reading,

Joss

xxx

Connect with me at www.josswoodbooks.com; Twitter: @josswoodbooks; Facebook: Joss Wood Author

JOSS WOOD

THE NANNY PROPOSAL

Special thanks and acknowledgment are given to
Joss Wood for her contribution to the
Texas Cattleman's Club: The Impostor miniseries.

Recycling programs
for this product may
not exist in your area.

ISBN-13: 978-1-335-97154-8

The Nanny Proposal

Copyright © 2018 by Harlequin Books S.A.

www.Harlequin.com

Printed in U.S.A.

Joss Wood loves books and traveling—especially to the wild places of Southern Africa. She has the domestic skills of a potted plant and drinks far too much coffee.

Joss has written for Harlequin KISS, Harlequin Presents and, most recently, the Harlequin Desire line. After a career in business, she now writes full-time. Joss is a member of the Romance Writers of America and Romance Writers of South Africa.

Books by Joss Wood

Harlequin Desire

Convenient Cinderella Bride

The Ballantyne Billionaires

His Ex's Well-Kept Secret
The Ballantyne Billionaires
The CEO's Nanny Affair
Little Secrets: Unexpectedly Pregnant
One Night to Forever

Texas Cattleman's Club: The Impostor

The Nanny Proposal

Visit her Author Profile page at Harlequin.com, or josswoodbooks.com, for more titles.

Dedicated to Rebecca Crowley,
who is leaving SA and heading home.
I'm going to miss you.
ROSACON is not going to be
the same without you!

Prologue

Eight months ago

Standing in the shadows of the balcony encircling the ballroom of the Texas Cattleman's Club, Kasey Monroe looked up at the clear night sky. Why had she thought attending a New Year's Eve Ball in Royal, Texas, knowing no one but Aaron Phillips—who might, or might not, become her new boss—was a good idea?

Aaron, as a member of the Texas Cattleman's Club, knew nearly everybody in the room. He'd introduced her to his gorgeous sister, Megan, and her equally good-looking husband, Will Sanders, CEO of Spark Energy Solutions. And while Aaron had made an effort to include her, she felt woefully out of place.

Even so, making small talk with strangers was still more fun than spending the night alone in her hotel room, obsessing about the party happening back in her home in Houston. Throwing a New Year's Eve bash was a tradition she and Dale had started the year they'd gotten engaged and, for the first time in five years, she wouldn't be playing hostess to their friends. Kasey couldn't help wondering what Michelle was doing tonight. When last had she and her oldest friend spent the special evening apart? A decade? More years than that? Kasey rested her champagne glass on her cheek. It had been six months since she'd caught Dale and Michelle together in what was, as they'd explained, a drunken encounter that meant nothing. Pure sex, fueled by too much booze and a line of coke. Their combination of sex, drugs and rock and roll had broken her heart and, while she felt like her heart was slowly patching itself back together, she still felt like a fool.

Her husband and her oldest and best friend... In a million years, she would never have imagined that scenario. Would she ever be able to trust anyone again?

Five! Four! Three! Two! One...! *Yeah, Happy New Year to me. Husband-less, friend-less, in a new town and among strangers.*

Oh, boo-hoo, Kasey thought, irritated by her bout of self-pity and taking a defiant gulp of her champagne. The last six months had been tough, sure, but ending a marriage should never be *fun*. But there was light at the end of the tunnel: her divorce was final, she had money in the bank and *options*.

One of those options was Aaron Phillips's intriguing proposal to become his executive assistant. Known as one of the most innovative and successful hedge fund managers in the country, Aaron didn't have a large client base, but that didn't matter because his clients were all mega wealthy. He worked out of his office within his palatial house on the outskirts of Royal and, as Aaron explained, thanks to the wonders of modern technology, she could do her job from either her home in Houston or here in Royal. He was demanding, Aaron told her, but he wasn't a micromanager and as long as she produced the results, she could set her own hours.

Kasey felt a spurt of excitement; a hefty salary, flexible hours and working out of her own space would give her life structure and, hopefully, would stop her from dwelling on her failed marriage and the loss of a childhood friend.

Kasey lightly whistled to catch the attention of the waiter hovering by the ballroom entrance. She held up her empty flute and within a minute had a fresh glass of bubbly in her hand. This new year would be better, Kasey vowed. She was a strong woman and she was not going to allow the past to define her. No matter what it took, she was going to put this all behind her and get back to the person she used to be. Fun, happy, positive.

Change had to happen and she was the only one who could implement those changes. She could start by accepting the position at AP Investments and re-locating to Royal. Even if she worked from home, a change of scenery, and leaving Houston, would be a good move. Tomorrow—*today*—was the start of a new year and a new life and, God knew, she desperately needed both.

Kasey looked into the ballroom and easily found Aaron's tall frame. She tipped her head, studying him. He was so very smart, so very well built and, pre-Dale, exactly the type of guy she'd look at twice. Or six times. Early to mid-thirties, with chestnut-brown hair cut short to tame the curl, he had the broad shoulders, long and powerful legs and narrow hips of a competitive swimmer. Unfathomable green eyes under—kill me now—wire-rimmed glasses. And light scruff covered his impressive jaw.

Sexy could be such a tame word, Kasey mused, feeling her stomach squirm. Then her skin tingled and she felt a slow burn that sent heat to that long-dead space between her legs. Wow...

Well, hello, sexual attraction. It's been a while.

In a room filled with some very fine eye candy, Aaron was handcrafted chocolate. Which meant, Kasey realized, the only way she could work for him would be virtually. There was no way she could spend eight or more hours a day with that gorgeous male specimen. At the *very* least, her keyboard would be perpetually covered in drool.

Kasey allowed a long slide of champagne to coat her throat and felt a small buzz. As if he could sense her eyes on him, Aaron slowly turned and scanned the ballroom. She really should look away, but Kasey, emboldened by the booze and the temptation of embarking on something different and a little bit wild, waited for his eyes to lock with hers. She'd met him twice before tonight and both times Aaron had been so professional and reticent, she'd found it impossible to read his emotions.

However, tonight there was desire and flat-out need in his eyes and on his face.

She turned around to check that there was no one behind her. No, she was alone and all that heat was for her. So...*hot damn.*

This certainly complicated the should-I-accept-his-job-offer question...

Kasey gripped the stem of her glass in a too tight grip and watched as Aaron walked, gracefully for such a big man, across the crowded floor. He was heading straight toward her, his eyes not leaving her face. Kasey swallowed and took another sip of champagne, hoping it would lubricate her dry mouth. One sip didn't help, neither did two. Hell, nothing would because a lava-hot man was looking at her like she was a pretty package he couldn't wait to unwrap.

Aaron stopped in front of her and lifted his hand. Kasey sucked in a breath, thinking he was about to touch her, then wrinkled her nose in disappointment when he plucked the champagne glass from her fingers and placed it on the edge of the railing. Aaron, still so close to her, looked down at her, his eyes drifting from her lips to her eyes.

"You look stunning, Kasey. Did I tell you that earlier?"

It had been so long since she'd been complimented on how she looked Kasey had no idea how to respond. When in doubt, and she was so in doubt, it was best to keep it simple.

"Thank you."

Unnerved by the warm appreciation in his eyes Kasey looked down at her tangerine halter-neck dress skimming her curves. Her two-inch heels just took her past Aaron's shoulder. He was a big man and his masculinity made her feel intensely feminine. Something else she was unfamiliar with.

"Happy New Year."

Kasey murmured the words back as a haunting melody drifted from the ballroom onto the balcony and swirled around them. Aaron's fingers touched her hip and Kasey felt heat pouring from him and burning through the thin fabric of her dress.

"Would you like to dance?" he asked, his deep voice raising goose bumps on her skin.

Aaron didn't wait for her reply. His hand slid around to rest on her lower back and he curled his other hand around hers, lifting it to hold it against his chest. Kasey felt his lips on her temple and wondered why, even though they were dancing outside, there was no fresh air. He was so warm, so solid, she thought as they swayed in place. Then Aaron's foot slid between hers and they were gliding across the empty balcony under the light of a Texas moon. The man sure could dance, Kasey mused as he spun her out and brought her back in, closer than before.

"You smell so good," Aaron whispered into her hair.

Her mouth curved into a smile. "I'm glad you approve."

Aaron pulled her hand up and raised her fingers to his mouth. His gentle kiss on the tips of her fingers sent heat skittering through her. "There's much I approve of, Kasey, and we both know that I'm not talking about your résumé and your references."

Kasey lifted her eyes to his face and saw his wry expression. She couldn't help noticing the desire in his eyes. And in his pants.

Aaron flicked the end of her hair with his index finger. "Since your arrival I've spent far too much time thinking about whether you'd feel as good as you look or whether your hair is as soft as I thought." He rubbed a strand of her shoulder-length hair between his fingers. "It is. And it's a fascinating color... I can't describe it. It's brown but not, red but not."

According to her stylist, her hair color was a rich, light auburn, but Michelle had always called it ginger spice. If all things were normal, if her best friend hadn't slept with her husband, Michelle would be the person she'd confide in about dancing with this sexy guy under the midnight blue Texas winter sky.

Don't think about her, them, the past!

Carpe diem, Monroe. Carpe diem...

Kasey laid her cheek on Aaron's chest and swayed along with him. *This is nice*, she thought. She felt relaxed and comfortable, *intensely* aroused, and pretty. She hadn't felt any of those things for a long time.

Aaron dropped her hand and his big arms pulled her closer. Every muscle in her body tensed as his hard length pushed into her stomach. Undeterred, he just gathered her against him, his hands flat against her lower back. "Relax, Kase, nothing is going to happen."

Damn, Kasey thought. It was the start of a new year and she really wanted something magical to happen. She wanted to feel his mouth on hers, to see if he tasted as delicious as he looked. She wanted those big, warm hands skating across her skin, wanted his mouth on her breast, on her stomach, maybe lower. She sighed. She wanted to feel what Aaron-induced pleasure felt like.

Bottom line? She wanted *him*.

"What if I want something to happen?" Kasey blurted out the words. She considered taking them back and forced herself not to. Aaron was a grown man. If he didn't want to get naked with her, he was adult enough to say so. But the action in his pants told her the thought had crossed his mind a time or two, as well.

This isn't a good idea, her overcautious brain insisted. *You want to work for him, you want to move to this festive town and to put some distance between you and your old life. Sleeping with your boss is not, on any planet or within any galaxy, a good idea. Besides, you're still sad, a little broken, still bruised.* Hopping into bed with Aaron, with *anyone*, wasn't a good idea. Feeling the twin urges of defiance and recklessness, Kasey's heart went to war with her head.

With Aaron, she didn't feel like the discarded wife, the foolish, naïve friend. In his arms, she remembered the confident woman she used to be. She felt desired and alive.

And they hadn't even got to the really good, rolling around naked, part yet.

Aaron put a little space between them. His expression turned contemplative, his eyes speculative. "What are you suggesting, Kasey?"

God, was he expecting her to draw him a picture? Suddenly feeling shy and out of her depth, Kasey placed her hands against his chest and tried to push him away, but he didn't move an inch.

"No, don't run away," Aaron said, his deep, husky voice soothing her agitation. "I just want us to be clear on what we are doing here. I want you to work for me, Kasey, and I don't want to lose you as an executive assistant because we want to scratch an itch."

She wanted to take the job. She did. The enormous salary would allow her to rent that fairy-tale cottage she'd fallen in love with in downtown Royal and would pay for her shoe and book habit. She wouldn't need to dip into her savings or the divorce settlement Dale agreed to pay for being a cheating douchebag dick. This job sounded interesting and challenging. But she really, really wanted to see what was under Aaron's perfectly tailored suit and blindingly white shirt.

"That's a sensible argument…" Kasey said, trailing off. Then she lifted her eyes to look into his. *Be brave, Kasey, take a chance. Start off the new year with a bang. Metaphorically.* And, maybe if the gods of good sex liked her, *literally.* "But on nights like these we aren't supposed to be sensible."

You're making a mistake—remember you can't trust your own judgment. You've made so many mistakes trusting men and people before.

Shut up, boring brain.

"One night, Kasey. A few hours to burn whatever we are feeling for each other out of our systems." Aaron's words echoed her thoughts. "I'm leaving for a skiing trip tomorrow and will only be back in Royal on the seventh. You can think about taking the job. If you do, this won't happen again. Ever. We'll be boss and employee."

Boss and employee. Kasey leaned back, knowing he'd hold her as she forced herself to think. Difficult to do when she was so desperate to say "to hell with it" and feel.

But she was an adult and she had to walk into this situation, his arms and his bed, with her eyes wide open and her head on straight.

A week's break would give them some time to clear their heads, to practice their "I've forgotten what you look like naked" attitude. They were adults, they could do this.

Kasey nibbled the inside of her cheek. She wanted to burn the memories of Dale away, to finally exorcise him from her life, and she wanted to do that with Aaron. He was fantastically good-looking, successful and smart. But, more than that, she instinctively liked him.

Consider him as a welcome-to-your-new-life gift to yourself, Monroe.

"You're killing me here, Kasey," Aaron muttered.

Kasey draped her arms over his shoulders as she eased closer to him. "One night, no expectations, and when we meet again, we'll be all business?"

Aaron nodded. "That's the way I'm looking at this."

Kasey smiled. "One question?"

Aaron closed his eyes, exaggerating his anguish. "Did I mention that you are killing me here?"

Kasey's laugh mingled with the music. "Your place or mine?"

One

Eight months later...

Aaron Phillips pulled up to the curb outside Kasey's rental home and cut the engine to his luxury, German-engineered SUV. The car was fine but he missed driving his Vanquish with its bucket seats and a million horses under the hood. But he was, as of yesterday, Savannah's guardian and that meant a solid, dependable, safe vehicle with a booster seat and top safety ratings.

God, what had Jason been drinking when he'd named him as Savannah's guardian and not their younger sister, Megan? What did he know about raising a little girl? Zero. And that was why he was parked outside the house of the woman he'd tried, as much as possible, to avoid for most of this year.

They talked often during the day, their Skype connection was pretty much always open and emails constantly bounced between them. But despite living in the same town, he hadn't laid eyes on her more than six times over the last eight months. Every one of those meetings had been an exercise in curtailing his impulse to scoop her up and carry her off to his bed.

That night, God, it was still burned into his brain. His memories of her were so strong that he could almost feel her endlessly, addictively soft and fragrant skin, hear the small murmurs of appreciation she made, taste the spicy sweetness of her mouth. As for those pretty, feminine places she hid from the world, they'd rocked his world.

She'd been so tight, warm…ridiculously responsive.

Aaron banged his forehead on the steering wheel, trying to push the image of Kasey, naked and wanton, whimpering with desire and begging for him to push her over the edge, from his brain.

How bizarre it was that the hottest sexual experience of his life had been with his executive assistant at the start of the year. His best and last sexual experience…

Eight. Months. God, he really needed to get laid.

But finding a date and some bedroom action was the last thing on his mind.

Aaron glared at Kasey's pretty cottage, with its pitched roof, pale green cladding and bright pink front door. The house stood in the shade of two live oaks and was enclosed by a whimsical wrought iron fence. He didn't want to do this, Aaron thought. He didn't want to walk up that path and pound on her door. He didn't want his brother, Jason, to be missing, presumed kidnapped, possibly dead.

From the moment he first held his hours-old niece he'd been wrapped around her now over developed baby finger. But he was the fun uncle, the rule breaker in contrast to Jason being the rule enforcer. He was the *stay up late and eat sweets before bedtime* guy, Jason was her *brush your teeth, chase away the monsters and eat your vegetables* dad. Now he had to assume—please God, only temporarily—the responsibility of this precious little person and he felt utterly out of his depth. And soul deep scared.

What the hell did he know about raising a girl? Precisely nothing.

Damn, he wanted life to roll back eight months, to be the man he was before that New Year's Eve ball when life was relatively simple and not the complicated crap storm it was at the moment.

Whining and wishing isn't going to get this done, Phillips. Neither is it going to change a damn thing. And you've survived life's crappy upheavals before...

Slamming the heavy car door, his long legs ate up the distance between his vehicle and Kasey's front door. At the entrance he hesitated, his fist hovering as he was slapped, again, by the images of his assistant, naked and sprawled across his bed, her amber eyes foggy with desire.

With her reddish-brown hair spread across his pillow, and her slim legs trembling with need—for him—she'd looked at him like he was the fulfillment of every fantasy she'd ever had. Then she'd whimpered and moaned, screamed his name, completely caught up in the throes of pleasure. They'd spent most of the night together and Kasey had been a full-fledged participant who gave as good as she got.

When he woke the next day, the start of a new year, she was gone, leaving nothing behind but her lingering scent in the air. Ten days later she'd walked back into his life as his executive assistant and neither of them ever made the smallest reference to that wonderful, crazy, sensation-soaked evening.

Didn't mean he didn't think about it. Often.

Aaron rested his forehead on the ridiculously pink door. He couldn't think about that night now, shouldn't be thinking about it all. He had a favor to ask of Kasey, and remembering her lusciously scented, velvety-soft skin and made-for-sin mouth was not helping matters.

Aaron ordered his junk to stand down, quickly adjusted himself and gave himself ten seconds to regain control. When he thought he was winning that battle, he rapped his fist against the door.

A minute passed and then another. Aaron glanced at his high-tech watch, his gift to himself for his thirty-third birthday, and frowned. It was after 9:00 a.m. Kasey should be up. His Saturday morning had already been jam-packed: he'd met with his lawyer, gathered the documentation to prove he was Savannah's legal guardian and filled Megan in on the big news.

It had been a brutal morning but, hell, that wasn't anything new. The past few months had been more of the same. It had started with the note Jason sent to Megan—accompanied by the urn containing Will's ashes—saying that he'd been with Will during the airplane crash and he needed time to grieve Will's death before returning home, something neither of them understood. Jason would never put his friend's death between him and his daughter, no matter how gutted he might be. Then Jason had stayed away, supposedly on business trips, and had failed time and time again to FaceTime with Savannah. As his frequent, albeit odd, emails had trickled to a stop, Aaron's and Megan's concern had mushroomed into genuine fear that something was *horribly* wrong.

Since Jason's disappearance—it had been too long to call it anything else—Savannah had been splitting her time between Aaron's and Megan's places. But they both agreed, with school starting soon, that Savannah needed permanence in her life. Megan was going through her own special type of hell—the man she'd married, and buried, was not actually the person she had thought he was. So until Jason came back, Savvie's place was with Aaron. *If* Jason came back…

His brother had to come back. He loved and adored his niece but Aaron wasn't ready to be a father to an almost-six-year-old girl who'd experienced more upheaval than any child should.

Jay, where the hell are you?

The front door opened and Aaron looked down into Kasey's heart-shaped, makeup-free face and, for an instant, he forgot how to breathe. She was dressed in a tank top, through which he could see the faint outline of her nipples, and the smallest pair of sleep shorts that skimmed the top of her thighs. His gaze drifted back up, drinking in those high cheekbones, that array of messy hair just grazing her shoulders, and those stunningly beautiful whiskey eyes groggy with sleep.

God, he wanted her. Still. Eight months of working with her hadn't cured him of that little affliction. He hadn't been so attracted to—*obsessed* with— a woman since Kate. And look how well that had turned out. His infatuation with Kate had had enormous consequences and was, in a roundabout way, responsible for his parents' death. His lack of a college degree, inability to trust and his emotional unavailability could also be traced back to *that* woman.

And here he was falling down that rabbit hole again, desperate to make Kasey his.

Your brother is in trouble. Your sister is heartbroken and confused. Your niece is a basket case and your world is falling apart. Is sex really what you should be thinking about, Phillips?

"Aaron…hi. Uh, what are you doing here?" Kasey asked, rubbing her fist in her eye.

Going slowly mad, Aaron silently answered. He looked over her head, easy to do since he was nearly a foot taller than her, into her sunny, colorful abode. "I need to talk to you."

Kasey pushed her fingers through her hair and Aaron noticed the way her breasts rose and fell with the movement. And a part of him rose…*sheesh.*

"Can it wait until Monday?"

"I wouldn't be here at nine on a Saturday morning if it could," Aaron retorted.

Kasey narrowed her eyes at his bark and he recognized her play-nice expression. Kasey was tough and strong-willed, and never hesitated to put him in his place if she felt he was being too pushy. He disliked doormats and her unwillingness to take crap from a work-obsessed, demanding boss was one of the things he liked best about her.

Sighing, he softened his tone. "Let me in, Kasey. Please."

She stepped back, and Aaron walked into her bright, airy cottage. After closing the front door behind him, he jammed his hands into the back pockets of his jeans. Her furniture looked used but comfortable, covered in checks and stripes in shades of the sea. Yellow and orange cushions and vibrant vases of flowers created splashes of color in the sunny room.

"Kitchen's that way." Kasey's bare arm brushed his as she pointed to a door behind him. "Make coffee, will you?"

"Where are you going?"

Kasey glanced down and Aaron noticed her flushed face. She gestured to her clothing. "Not exactly the outfit I need my boss to see me in."

Aaron started to remind her that he'd seen her in much less but at the last minute pulled the words back. For eight months they'd pretended that night had never happened and mentioning it now, when she was halfway to naked, wasn't appropriate.

His brother was missing and his niece needed him.

He was also one of the few people who knew that the man he'd thought was his old friend and brother-in-law was an impostor. Plus, he was trying to support his sister, whose life was even more of a tangled mess than his.

Which meant sex with Kasey should be the *last* thing on his mind.

Aaron swore and scrubbed his hands over his face. When he opened them again, Kasey was walking away from him. He ordered himself not to follow her—but, hot damn, those shorts did *not* cover her butt cheeks.

Coffee, Aaron thought. Coffee was the only thing that made sense right now. He slipped into Kasey's tiny kitchen, thinking he was far too big for this dollhouse. His house was huge—eight thousand square feet and seven bedrooms—but as he'd told Jason, who'd sarcastically called his house "the Shack," at six-three he was a big guy and he liked a lot of space.

A few minutes later Aaron saw Kasey standing in the doorway, wearing a pair of knee-length, cut-off denim shorts and a blue, white and red striped top. She was shoeless, her toes ending in slashes of hot pink. She'd brushed her hair, washed her face and, judging by the peppermint smell, brushed her teeth. Her face was still free of makeup, but she rarely wore much: her eyelashes were long and thick and her mouth a natural, deep pink. As always, she took his breath away.

"I need your help," Aaron stated, trying to get his mind off the bed down her hall.

Kasey picked up her mug, sipped and lifted her finely arched, dark eyebrows. "Okay." She glanced down at her clothes and grimaced. "Do we need to go to the office? Must I change?"

"Not necessary," Aaron told her. "You're fine as you are."

Kasey waved her coffee cup in a silent gesture for him to continue.

Should he tell her? Was he doing the right thing? Aaron wrestled with his doubt. He didn't trust anyone, not fully, but he needed Kasey's help and that meant sharing classified information, something he wasn't comfortable doing. He'd learned, the hard way, to keep his secrets, both business and personal, close to his chest.

"I'm trusting you not to repeat this, Kasey."

She nodded and Aaron continued. "It's a long, tangled story. You met Will at the ball. How much do you know about him?"

Kasey replied immediately, her business brain moving into high gear. "CEO of Spark Energy Solutions, a company with ties to oil, gas and solar. Recently passed away?"

"Yeah. A while ago, Will and Rich Lowell, his best friend, were in Mexico and they got caught up in a boating accident. Long story short, the boat exploded and we were told Rich died. Except that wasn't what happened. Rich escaped the brunt of the blast and Will's body was never recovered."

Kasey waited for him to continue.

"This is where it gets odd… Rich presumed Will

died in that blast and he returned to Royal—but he returned as Will. Acting as Will, Rich took over Will's life and his business. Married my sister. Then, a few months back, Rich, still pretending to be Will, faked his own death... Following me so far?"

Kasey looked dazed. He didn't blame her; it was a hell of a story. "Meanwhile, the real Will also did not perish in that boat explosion."

"Seriously? So where was he while Rich was assuming his identity?"

"He was in Mexico, recovering from his injuries. He's now back in town, laying low and quietly trying to unravel the mess." Aaron released a breath. "My brother, Jason, is Will's good friend and worked closely with him at Will's energy company, SES."

"Your brother didn't notice the difference between the real and the fake Will?" Kasey asked, sounding skeptical.

"Remember that boating accident? Acting as Will, Rich claimed he'd been badly injured, that he'd needed reconstructive surgery to both his face and vocal chords. Jason took his words at face value. Will and Rich had the same coloring and build, and they looked a lot alike, so none of us ever thought, not for a minute, that Rich wasn't who he said he was."

Kasey looked puzzled. "Okay, but I still don't understand how this relates to me doing a favor for you."

"Getting there... As I said, Jason worked for Will and he's gone missing. It's been two months since anyone has spoken to, or seen, him."

Sympathy crossed Kasey's lovely face. "I'm so sorry, Aaron. That must be awful."

That was one word for it. "My sister received a letter from him saying that he needed time away to recover from Will's death. But that letter was fake—it definitely wasn't his handwriting. Besides, no matter how upset Jason was, he would never abandon his little girl."

Aaron heard the harsh note in his voice and tried to tone it down, to find his control. "He's a devoted dad and he'd never neglect Savannah for this long. There have been emails, but on other trips Jason never connected with Savvie through emails—she's too little— he always FaceTimed with her." Aaron tossed his cold coffee into her sink and linked his hands around the back of his neck. "In short, Jason is officially missing, presumed kidnapped." He forced the words out. "It's possible that he's dead."

Kasey lifted her fist to her mouth, her eyes wide with shock mixed with horror. "God, Aaron."

He imagined himself in her arms, soaking in her strength, leaning on her, emotionally, for a minute, maybe two. But that wasn't what he allowed himself— he didn't fall apart, he couldn't. He had to be strong. For Jason. For Megan. For Savannah.

"Savvie is five, nearly six, and has been bouncing between Megan, my sister's house and mine. I remember Jason naming me as her guardian after her mom died a year or so back but I never expected to have to take full responsibility for her." First her mom, then her dad. No wonder Savannah looked and sounded shell-shocked. "I'm picking her up from my sister Megan's soon, but, while I can handle the occasional sleepover or a weekend here and there, she's going to be with me full-time."

Well, here went nothing. "I need reinforcements and I was hoping that you would, um, lend me a hand with her."

Kasey looked like he'd asked her to play with acid-covered playing cards. "Aaron, I'm your executive assistant, not a babysitter. You have an enormous disposable income, hire a nanny!"

A stranger in his house? No. Aaron folded his arms, prepared to argue. "On your résumé, you said that you spent a year in France as an au pair. And I'll double your salary if you take on the extra workload."

Kasey still looked doubtful.

"Yeah, I could hire a nanny but you're young, warm, and I think she'd relate to you better. I just need to get through the next couple of weeks, someone to help me until she goes to school. Then I'll make another plan," Aaron added.

"What about your sister? Can't she help you?"

Megan was trying to unravel her own messy life and while he knew that she could occasionally help out, she wasn't available on a continual basis. "Megan has her own issues she's dealing with."

Aaron looked at Kasey, almost prepared to grovel. "I trust you, Kasey. I trust you with my business." Okay, that was a small lie. He trusted her as much as he could and only with parts of his business.

"The hell of it is that I need you. So, will you help me?"

* * *

I need you...

Kasey was still trying to make sense of his words when her cell phone buzzed with an incoming call. Seeing Michelle's name on her screen brought the usual wave of longing and disgust, regret and anger, so she did what she always did and let the call go to voice mail. She couldn't deal with her former best friend right now. She wasn't sure whether she ever could.

Kasey looked at Aaron, who dominated her small kitchen. She could see the worry in his deep green eyes; it was also etched into the grooves edging his masculine but still sexy mouth, painted in the dark circles under his eyes. He also looked like he'd lost weight, which in Aaron's case meant that he'd dropped muscle since there wasn't an inch of fat on him. She'd checked.

Despite working virtually and only seeing him within the confines of a computer monitor, she'd noticed that he was worried and, day-by-day, she saw his tension levels ratcheting up. Thanks to that amazing, glorious night that could not be mentioned, they were very careful to keep their relationship strictly professional, so she'd avoided asking him what was wrong and whether she could help.

And that raised the question, did she want to help? Should she help? She rather liked being on the outside looking in; it felt safer that way. But lately she'd started to think that maybe it was time to come out of her self-imposed hermit lifestyle, to start engaging with the world again. Meet some new people and, maybe, make a friend or two.

She wasn't looking for a new best friend or a new lover—she didn't trust herself or her judgment to go that far—but sharing a meal with a nice man or a cup of coffee with a girlfriend might be fun. But, God, she was so out of practice. She needed to dust off her social skills; Aaron was the only person she spoke to on a regular basis and that was all about business.

Looking after Savannah would pull her out of her rut and make her interact with someone new, even if she was only five years old. But she had to be careful, she'd made a promise to herself to protect what was left of her heart and she couldn't afford to become emotionally attached to anyone, let alone a little girl who'd lost her mom and maybe—God, she prayed not—her dad.

"It's a temporary gig, Kasey. Just until we find our feet," Aaron said.

Kasey tapped her nails against her fake granite countertop, fighting the urge to say no, to crawl back into the security of her quiet and lonely life. If she kept to herself, then no one could hurt her…

But they were talking about a little girl. What harm could she do?

Kasey thought she could handle Savannah but she had to remember that she came as a package deal with Aaron. And she definitely *couldn't* handle him!

To give herself some time to think, Kasey lifted her phone to her ear to listen to Michelle's message. "So, I know you're not too happy with me at the moment but it's been a while since we spoke. Kasey, we need to resolve our issues. I need to say sorry for my oops and you need to forgive me."

Oops? That was what her childhood friend was calling sleeping with her husband? An *oops*? Holy hell, now she'd heard it all.

"Anyway, I've tracked you down and I'm driving to Royal to see you. I should be there later this morning. And we're going to talk, Kasey. You can't keep running from me. I'm staying for the weekend, possibly longer if I can't get through to you, and we're going to thrash this out."

Like hell she was. Kasey's eyes flew to the clock on the wall—it was already ten and Michelle was super punctual. In fact, she was often early. She bit her lip and thought fast. "Would me helping you with Savannah mean me moving into your house?"

"It would make sense," Aaron replied, his voice as neutral as Switzerland.

Two hours ago the thought of sleeping down the hall from the hottest man in Royal would've sent her running for the hills. But dealing with Michelle, rehashing their torrid past, was more terrifying than dealing with a little girl and Kasey's raging but hopefully well-hidden lust for her boss.

Sold, Kasey thought. Michelle would arrive in Royal, not find her at home and, after a day, maybe two—because she had a low attention span and was easily bored—she'd hightail it back to Houston.

"I'll help you with Savannah this weekend, as a trial run," Kasey said. Not giving Aaron time to respond, she whipped around and headed down the hallway to her bedroom. Stepping into her tiny walk-in closet, she stood on her tiptoes and lunged for the suitcase on the highest shelf. A big, burly man from the moving company had placed it there for her; she'd thought it would be months before she needed it again.

Kasey jumped, her fingers grazing the edge of the suitcase, which wobbled and stayed put. Dammit, she hated being short. Kasey took a step back and hit a solid wall of muscle. She tensed and her brain ordered her traitorous body not to push her butt into his groin.

Aaron's chest connected with her back as his arm reached for the suitcase, easily lifting the case off the shelf. His muscles bulged as he held it in the air and Kasey felt his hard body press up against her back, thought she felt his warm breath fanning her neck. Kasey stared at a pile of her T-shirts, telling herself that she couldn't—*shouldn't*—turn around. That it wasn't a good idea to rise to her toes and slam her mouth against his.

Kasey heard Aaron's muffled curse in her ear, heard the suitcase hit the floor and then Aaron's big hands were on her shoulders and he spun her around to face him. She caught a glimpse of green fire in his eyes before he abruptly stepped back, holding up his hands, broad palms facing her, his chest heaving.

"Kasey." Her name was both a warning and a plea. As her boss he wouldn't initiate anything but she could, she had to. Kasey placed her fingers on his jaw and reached up to touch her mouth to his.

They both needed this connection…

Aaron made an appreciative sound in the back of his throat as his tongue slipped past her teeth to slide against hers, long, sexy strokes that heated her skin and made her head swim.

She'd missed this. She'd missed being the object of a man's desire, of being held and kissed, of feeling feminine and powerful and so, so sexy. Despite only sharing a few, pleasure-saturated hours with him, she'd missed Aaron. When she thought of pleasure and sex and desire, his was the face that came to mind, his hands, his kisses, his touch. And hadn't that been the point of that night so long ago?

She shouldn't be enjoying his kiss so much, her hands shouldn't be exploring the hard muscles under his bare skin. She shouldn't be pressing her breasts into his chest. And she most certainly should *not* be twisting her tongue around his, making those sounds of appreciation low in her throat.

My God. What was she thinking? Rationality filtered in as she remembered that he was her *boss*. What they'd had was a onetime thing. She was moving into his house to avoid Michelle, to help him with his niece, not to warm his bed. *Pull away, Kasey. Now.*

Just five minutes more…

Aaron jerked his mouth off hers, his fingers digging into her hips. He rested his forehead against hers and she was pleased to see that his face was flushed, that he, also, was short of breath. That they were both struggling for control. At least she wasn't alone in this madness.

"Kase—"

Kasey yanked her hands out from underneath his shirt and pushed the heels of her hands in her eye sockets. This man had the ability to shut down her synapses, to trip the power supply to her brain.

Kasey looked down at her bare toes, noticed a small chip in the nail polish on her middle toe. She didn't want to have this conversation but she needed to make sure of what she was walking into. "I'm going to be living and working in your house, Aaron. For a couple of nights at the very least."

She lifted her head to see Aaron's "Yeah, so?" look.

Man, this was embarrassing, but because her entire marriage had been based on lies, Kasey chose honesty over embarrassment. "Are you expecting more when I move in with you? Because that's not going to happen."

Irritation flickered in his eyes. "I never, for one moment, thought it would. You're still my employee and I'm still your boss."

"I initiated that kiss but you were as into it as I was, Aaron."

Irritation morphed into frustration and his muttered curse bounced off the walls of her bedroom. "I know. But we had an agreement and that agreement still stands."

"Then why didn't we stop?" Why was she pushing him on this? What did she want from him? Kasey didn't know. What she should be doing is laughing it off, ignoring buzz of sexual attraction between them. This was akin to poking a bear with a stick...

"I don't know what your excuse is but I had five feet plus of pure perfection pressed up against me. When you haven't been laid for eight long months, temptation is hard to resist!"

Kasey stared at him, trying to process his words. He thought she was perfect? He hadn't had sex since her? He was gorgeous and ripped, and she knew that when he walked down the street women stared at him, lust and appreciation in their eyes.

Aaron cursed again and started to walk away. At the door, he turned and those piercing green eyes pinned her to the floor. "My life is a mess, Kasey, and I don't need any more complications."

Kasey and reality collided with a hard thump and she nodded, embarrassed. "I shouldn't have kissed you. I'm sorry if I made you feel uncomfortable."

Aaron looked down at his tented pants and lifted an eyebrow. "In more ways than one." He then released a heavy sigh. "You started it but I got into it so we're both, equally, at fault and I apologize."

Aaron placed his hands on his hips. "Can we keep it simple? You're my assistant and temporary nanny, that's it."

Yeah, that was it. That was all it could be. It didn't matter that they had enough sexual chemistry to ignite the room, they needed to keep their distance. She respected Aaron's big brain—and, because she was still a woman, she also appreciated his very excellent body—but she was not prepared to jeopardize her job or to allow her heart to hope.

"So you're with me on this? From this moment on,

our relationship stays strictly professional?" Aaron was giving her that steely eyed, hard-ass look he frequently used when dealing with a complicated work issue.

He was right. It was essential that they didn't make this situation any more complicated than it needed to be. Kasey capitulated to common sense. "It's a deal."

Two

From the balcony off his office on the second floor of his house, Aaron watched Kasey pull to a stop at the back entrance. Jumping out of her SUV, Kasey shoved her sunglasses to the top of her head and opened the back door. Aaron watched his niece leave the vehicle, all dark hair, sad eyes and long legs. So young, she'd experienced more upheaval than most people would in a lifetime. Aaron felt his stomach cramp and closed his eyes. *Crap, Jay, where the hell are you? What more can I do to find you?*

Look after Savvie, bro, he heard Jason's voice say in his head. *If you want to do right by me, look after my precious, precious daughter.*

I am. She's in my care until you come home, just as you wanted.

"I left a snack on the kitchen counter for you, Savannah." Kasey's voice floated up to him and Aaron opened his eyes to see her place her hand on Savannah's shoulder. "Then you can have a quick swim before your ballet lessons. That work?"

It was Wednesday and Kasey, without further discussion, was still here and doing a fabulous job with his niece. Her natural warmth and her non-pushy attitude endeared her to Savannah. They'd clicked the moment they'd met.

He tended to avoid talking to Savannah about Jason but Kasey faced that issue head-on, allowing the little girl to express her fears, holding her when she cried and answering her many questions about where her dad could be. Kasey answered Savannah as honestly as she could, never giving the child false hope or making any promises that no one could fulfill.

Savannah wasn't happy, far from it, but when she was around Kasey, she was more cheerful than he'd seen her in weeks. Both Savannah and Kasey were now living with him on a full-time basis. Sure, Savvie had been a frequent visitor to his house but it still felt strange to share his space with a woman and a girl, to find hair ties on his kitchen table and dolls on the floor. Kasey's perfume floated through the house and there were flowers on the dining table and on the desk she used in the corner of his office. Music filled his house and his fridge was filled with girlie foods like low fat yogurt, frilly lettuce and hummus.

"Will you swim with me, Kasey?" Savannah asked, and Aaron tuned back into their conversation.

"Sure thing, sweetheart. I just need to check in with Aaron to see if he has any work for me," Kasey replied.

Aaron saw the flash of disappointment cross Savannah's face. With her dark brown hair and green eyes, she was going to be beautiful. Hell, if he discounted the fear and sadness, she already was.

"Nothing that can't wait. Maybe I'll join you two," Aaron said, resting his arms on the railing of the balcony. Savannah's head shot up and she managed a small smile before running into the house. Kasey stood in place, her arms folded across the cotton fabric of her sleeveless sundress. He could see the concern in her eyes, could read her thoughts as easily as he could the stock market.

"You don't have to join us," Kasey said.

"It's fine. I'm hot and I need a break." Aaron knew she worried that shedding most of their clothes would crack open the door that kept their mutual attraction under lock and key.

It was a swim, he wanted to tell Kasey. They'd have an almost-six-year-old to chaperone them. Aaron ran his hand across his face, reluctantly admitting that if he and Kasey found themselves in a pool alone, their clothes would be shed in world-record-breaking speed. They were *that* combustible.

Despite it only being a couple of days, living together in the same house was torture. They shared his office. They shared their meals. They were constantly in close proximity and, when he went to bed, he was deeply conscious that Kasey was across the hall in the bedroom next to Savannah's. Every night he needed to talk himself out of slipping into her bed, of losing himself in her for an hour or two or most of the night.

He tried, he really did, not to think about her like that but at night, when the lights were off, he was ambushed by memories of how she felt…

God. Boss of the Year he was not.

Really, didn't he have better things to do than fantasize about his employee? Aaron turned away and walked back into his cool study, dropping into his leather chair. He had too many responsibilities to allow himself to be distracted by Kasey with her endless curves and catlike amber eyes.

First and foremost, he needed to find out what the hell had happened to Jason. His gaze drifted to the silver frame on his desk: two little boys held fish up to the camera, their toothy grins wide and free. He and Jason were only a year apart and nobody knew his brother better than he did. Yeah, they'd fought and they'd competed—girls, sports, business—but they were brothers, and blood always, always, came first. He'd been Jason's best man at his wedding, had handed him cigars and gotten him drunk when he'd become a dad. He'd kept his hand on his back and been a pillar of strength for him when he'd buried Ruth.

It had been more than two months since he'd heard from Jay and Aaron knew in his gut that something was wrong. Desperately wrong.

His brother was work obsessed but he'd never neglected Savannah. He was a good dad and, if Savannah was staying with Aaron or with Megan while Jay traveled, he made it a point to connect with his daughter every day, morning and night. Something terrible had to have happened because Aaron knew Jason would move heaven and earth to speak to his child.

Cole Sullivan, the PI his friend Will had hired, also believed that Jason was in deep crap. The note Megan had received—supposedly from Jason, stating he needed space to deal with Will's death—had been proved, through handwriting analysis, not to be Jason's.

Aaron could've told them that. Jason was a Phillips. They didn't run away from their responsibilities. His brother would never turn his back on his daughter. He wouldn't ignore his family's entreaties to get in touch just so he could wallow in his own pain.

No, something was very, very wrong.

Aaron heard the door to his study open and Kasey walked in, heading for her desk in the corner. Instead of taking a seat, she bent from the waist down to peer at her monitor, her sundress perfectly delineating her heart-shaped ass, the same ass he'd slid his hands under to haul her against him as he'd lost himself in her eight months ago. He couldn't help his eyes traveling down as her short dress rode up in the back, allowing him a look at her slim, tanned thighs. Those spectacular legs had encircled his hips, had been draped over his shoulders as he'd—

God, he needed to get laid. Eight months was far too damn long, but whenever he considered finding a date, Kasey's face popped into his head. He didn't want sex with some random female. He wanted Kasey. Which posed a problem, because the woman worked for him and was helping him, temporarily, to raise his niece. He couldn't jeopardize either situation, or his honor, for sex. His neglected junk violently disagreed.

There was something—damn, what was the word?—*homey* about having his house and life invaded by two intensely girlie girls. Savvie's occasional visits didn't carry the same punch as having them here 24/7. The dolls and smells and music were comforting, and hearing feminine voices and the occasional trill of laughter made his house feel more like a home than the huge tomb he usually inhabited.

Aaron rubbed the back of his neck and reminded himself that this wasn't normal. Normal was Jay back at home with Savvie, Kasey in her house, he in his. He couldn't afford to get attached. All his relationships, romantic or not, tended to be messy and, as an added bonus, the people he loved tended to leave him. Sometimes both at the same time. No, it was better to stay emotionally detached.

But that resolve didn't help him with his need-to-get-laid problem.

Kasey stood straight and Aaron quickly looked up, glad that his desk hid his arousal. There were certain things Kasey did not need to know and his craving for her was one of them. "Aaron, I'm falling behind."

"How can I help?"

"Can you do Savvie's ballet run? I could use that time to catch up here."

Aaron nodded. It would do him good to get out of the house, away from the monitors and making financial decisions involving hundreds of millions of dollars. That took its toll and he could feel a stress headache building between his eyes.

Kasey opened the right-hand drawer to his desk and lobbed him a bottle of aspirin. "Take two and come for a swim, it'll help you unwind."

Aaron opened the bottle, shook the pills into his hand and tossed them into his mouth. He dry-swallowed the pills and ignored Kasey's wince. "How did Savvie do at day camp today?"

Kasey picked up a pen and threaded it through her fingers, something she often did. "She was better, I think. She told me that some boy brought in his guinea pig and that some of the girls were scared of it, but she'd loved it." Kasey sent him a look and he knew that something big was coming his way, something he might not like. "I think you should buy her a puppy."

Yep, there it was. "Kasey, do we not have enough on our hands without adding a puppy to the craziness?"

"She loves animals, Aaron, and she needs something to love."

"She has me and Megan."

"Her mom and dad have both left her, so she doesn't trust other adults not to do the same," Kasey argued, stubbornness settling into her expression.

She was not going to let this go. Damn, they were going to get a puppy, sometime soon.

He thought he should at least try to change her

mind. "She's not old enough to handle the responsibility of looking after a dog, Kasey."

"This isn't about being responsible, Aaron. It's about her having something in her life she can hold on to," she reiterated. "Having something to love. Everyone needs someone or something to love and, God knows, dogs are a hundred times more reliable than humans."

And didn't that statement, Aaron thought as she walked out of the room, give him a glimpse into her soul.

Kasey stomped down the hallway and ducked into her room. Kicking off her sandals, she immediately walked over to the French doors and flung them open, allowing the heat of the hot Texas day to slide into her bedroom. For the last year or so she'd felt perpetually cold—a physical reaction to emotional pain—so she didn't mind a little heat.

Kasey rested her head against the door frame and closed her eyes. She was exhausted, which was the only reason she'd allowed those revealing words to leave her lips. *Everyone needs someone or something to love and, God knows, dogs are a hundred times more reliable than humans...*

And wasn't that the truth. Kasey looked at the small picture on her bedside table, her gaze focusing on the mixed breed she held in her arms. She'd found Rufus in Cleveland, the puppy half-starved, for food and affection. Because her parents were generally oblivious, she'd managed to keep him hidden until they moved to... God, what city came after Cleveland? Cincinnati? Boston? It was all a blur. But she did remember the screaming fight she'd had with her parents, that if they insisted on lugging her from place to place, school to school, then the least they could do was let her have one friend, even if it was a canine. Ru, like her, had endured the moves and loved the summer holidays at her grandparents' house in Houston. All she'd wanted was a stable home life, a place to settle down in, and she'd found that for three months of the year, in Houston.

Years later she'd believed that she'd found her place, her permanent home with Dale. Yeah, that hadn't turned out the way she expected it to.

Kasey walked over to the king-size bed covered in expensive, white Egyptian cotton and picked up her phone. There were two missed calls from Michelle, one from Dale. Knowing it was more of the same old, same old, she blew out a frustrated breath and tossed her phone back onto the bed.

Dale and Michelle were in a race to win her back. Both wanted to be the first to earn her forgiveness. They were both sorry…they'd made a mistake…could she forgive them?

Hell, no.

Their infidelity had not only left her unable to fathom being in a relationship again, but also riddled her with insane trust issues. She'd spent the last eight months rebuilding her life. She was starting to feel vaguely normal and she was so much stronger. She liked her job, she liked Royal and she liked not having to deal with their neediness and drama. At some point she'd have to meet with them, face them, but today wasn't that day. Tomorrow wasn't looking good for them, either.

"I'm ready, Kasey."

Kasey turned and smiled at Savannah, who stood in her open doorway, dressed in a pink-and-purple swimsuit, her swimming goggles high on her head.

Savannah noticed that Kasey was still wearing her sundress and her expression turned to resignation, her face crumpling. "Okay, well…if you're not going to swim, then I'll just go to my room."

So much pain, Kasey thought, her heart flipping over. Savannah was nearly six but she expected adults to disappoint her.

"Honey, I was just woolgathering. Of course I'm going to swim with you." Kasey walked over to the dresser and pulled open the top drawer. Yanking out her swimsuits, she held them up. "The blue racer or the orange bikini?"

Savannah, because she was a mini fashionista, tipped her head, giving the question her complete attention. "The orange bikini."

Damn, Kasey silently thought. The bikini was modest, but it was still four triangles and she didn't feel comfortable showing Aaron that much skin.

A little too late, Monroe, considering the man once managed to kiss every inch of your skin.

But she wasn't thinking about that, about him, about how his touch made her combust from the inside out… She remembered the taste of his mouth, his skin, how his fingers trailed over her—

No! Stop!

Enough. They'd had their one insanely hot night together and, as mind-blowing as it had been, it could never be repeated again.

She was permanently unavailable and he was her super-professional boss, so getting worked up about showing a little flesh was just…stupid. Apart from that kiss in her house days ago, Aaron never made any reference to what they'd done, how they'd done it and how hot it had been. He was so inscrutable that some days she even doubted that night had ever happened and she sometimes wondered whether Aaron naked was a very erotic, very sexy, figment of her imagination.

"Kasey!"

Kasey blinked and looked at Savannah, hands on her tiny hips, her green eyes frustrated. She clapped her hands and made a shooing motion. "You are wool-grabbing again."

Kasey started to correct her but smiled instead. "You're right, I am."

God, she really, really liked this kid. She had to be careful. After her marriage imploded, she'd promised herself she wasn't going to form emotional attachments again. She didn't trust herself enough to do that. Because trust and attachment led to a shattered heart and hers was only just starting to heal.

Aaron sat on a pool lounger a few yards from the pool. Kasey and Savannah were sitting in the water, on the wide, first step of the massive pool. Nearly every doll Savannah owned was in the pool with them and Kasey was helping Savannah to teach them to swim.

Kasey, long-limbed and slim, flipped a chubby plastic doll onto its back to make it float. Savannah, sitting between Kasey's legs, guided the doll through the water, her one hand on Kasey's thigh. They were lost in their own conversation, oblivious to his presence.

At one point in his life, while he'd still been at college, he'd dreamed of this: a big house, money in the bank, a hot wife and a cute kid. He'd been happy to play the field, but in the back of his mind he'd always been on the lookout for "the One." His perfect match. Instant recognition of his soul mate. God, for a guy who'd always had nerves of steel when it came to finance, he'd been such a damn romantic.

There was nothing romantic about being the direct cause of his parents' car accident or having his fiancée run off with his client list six months after opening their investment firm together, nearly bankrupting him in the process. Kate had been six years older than him, sophisticated, and he'd hung on her every word. He'd believed her when she'd insisted he was bright enough to make it without completing his last semester of college, that he didn't need his degree in finance and that he needed to concentrate on their business. So in love with her, he'd dropped out of college, breaking his parents' hearts and ultimately causing their deaths.

Afterward he'd flung himself into their business, working crazy hours to get their company off the ground, to distance himself from the grief. How had

Kate repaid him? The month after he'd made his first five-million trade, she'd visited every one of their clients and told them that she was the one reading the markets, that she was concerned about his emotional health, his youth. His clients, scared to risk their money on such a young trader, had moved their portfolios to Kate. He'd been left with the three clients she hadn't been brave enough to approach: his brother, Will Sanders and Megan. He'd taken his life savings, Megan's and Jason's modest investments and Will's larger investment, and made them all a damned fortune. His former clients, who had lost money with Kate, had reached out to him, asking him to manage their money again.

Because loyalty was everything to him, Aaron had refused. Besides, by that point—and thanks to Will's word-of-mouth advertising—he had more, far richer, clients than he could handle.

God, if only his parents had trusted his decision. If only they hadn't freaked and jumped into that car ten minutes after he'd told them he was dropping out of school. If only they hadn't driven through the night to confront him at Berkeley. If they had trusted him, just a little…

His heart had splintered into a million pieces when his parents died and what was left had been decimated by Kate's deceit. He would've given Kate everything. But she'd screwed him over, big-time, and, ten years later, his heart still wasn't capable of giving or receiving love.

Did Savannah sense that? Was that why she was

so reserved around him? Did she subconsciously realize that he had nothing to give? God, he hoped not. If
Jason— God...if his brother didn't come back, could
he love Savannah the way she deserved to be loved,
the way a little girl *needed* to be loved? He wasn't
so sure...

*Dammit, Jay, you'd better be doing everything you
can to get yourself back here! I can't do this... Savvie
needs you. She needs her dad.*

And, hell, I need my brother.

He should be working, Aaron thought. There were
markets to check, decisions to make. But he could
take another five minutes to sit in the afternoon sun
and soak up some rays. He tried to sit still but, feeling antsy, he reached for his cell and dialed Cole Sullivan's number.

The private investigator had assured him that he
was doing everything he could to find Jason. But
surely there was something Aaron could do, as well?
Because, sure as hell, sitting around in the sun while
his brother was missing wasn't it. Guilt, acidic and
bitter, burned his tongue and the roof of his mouth.

"Sullivan."

Aaron asked whether Cole had any news.

"Nothing concrete since the last time we spoke,
Aaron."

Nothing concrete... Did that mean Cole had found
something? "Do you have a hunch about what happened?"

"I have nothing *concrete*, Aaron," Cole repeated.

"I make it a policy not to share my hunches or suppositions without anything to back them up."

Crap. Aaron gripped the bridge of his nose and ignored the burning in his eyes. "What can I do, Cole? Just tell me. I need to do something…the waiting is killing me."

"If there is anything, I'll let you know. Hang tough, Aaron. I'm hoping to have some solid answers for you soon."

"Okay. Keep me updated."

"You will be the second person I call," Cole promised him.

Aaron wanted to protest but remembered that Cole was working for Will. He wasn't calling the shots, wasn't Cole's client, and that burned him. He liked being in charge, but he was somewhat pacified by the knowledge that he was in the loop, that he'd get the information as soon as Will did. Besides, he instinctively trusted Cole. He knew he was doing everything he could to track down Jason.

Aaron saw the tiny feet next to his size thirteens and slowly lifted his head to look into Savannah's worried face. They shared the same green eyes, he thought, the Phillips chin.

"Were you talking to someone about my daddy?" Savannah demanded, fear and worry in her eyes.

Aaron felt like he was looking into his own soul. He thought about lying, then decided she deserved, and needed, the truth. "Yeah, Savvie, I was."

"Is he coming home soon?" Savannah asked, her bottom lip wobbling.

Aaron took her hand in his and sat straighter. His gut clenched at the mixture of hope and fear he saw in her eyes. "I don't know, honey. We're trying to find him."

"Something's wrong, Uncle Aaron. Daddy always calls me and it's been so long."

Tears just made the green of her eyes more brilliant.

Aaron reached up and touched her cheek with the back of his knuckle. "I know, honey. I'm worried, too." He gestured to his phone, conscious of Kasey standing a few feet behind Savannah, her body stiff with tension. Did she think he should be more up-beat? That he should be more optimistic? Was this one of those times when he should be lying his ass off?

He met her eyes and saw her concern for Savvie. She was clearly holding herself back, resisting the urge to sweep the little girl into her arms and soothe away her pain.

Aaron was grateful for her reticence. This conversation, as hard as it was, was the first real conversation he'd had with Savannah since she'd moved in full-time.

He picked up his phone and tossed it from one hand to another. "The man I was just talking to? His name is Mr. Sullivan, and his job is to find people who have gone missing."

"Will he find my daddy?"

Aaron lifted his broad shoulders in a weary shrug. "He's trying, honey. I just called him to ask him if I could help him, but there's nothing I can do. I would if I could, but this is his job."

Savannah moved so that she was standing between

his legs. Aaron slid his arm around her, being careful to keep his touch gentle. His eyes burned when she laid her head on his shoulder. "Your job is to look after me… I heard you saying that to Kasey."

"It *is* my job. Nobody is more important to your dad than you and he'd want me to make sure that you are safe."

Savannah pushed her face into his neck and he felt her warm breath on his skin. "I miss him, Uncle Aaron."

"I do, too, Savvie." Aaron rested his cheek against her head and closed his eyes. *God, Jay, where the hell are you?*

He heard Kasey's footsteps and lifted his head to look at her. Her expression was pure sympathy and he managed a quick, half-baked smile.

Kasey placed a hand on Savvie's shoulder. "Hey, sweet pea, if you don't run upstairs now to change, you're going to be late for your ballet lesson."

Savannah pulled back and her eyes widened. "And if anyone is late, Mrs. Pitman goes red and her mouth goes all funny." Savannah made a face and both he and Kasey laughed at her squinty eyes and pursed lips. "I'm going to change real fast, Kasey."

"You do that, Savvie. Aaron is going to take you to your lesson and he'll pick you up, okay?"

Savannah looked at Aaron and, for a long moment, he thought she might demand that Kasey take her. "'Kay," she said before running across the outdoor living area and into the house.

Aaron stood and looked at Kasey, who was wrapping a piece of gauzy fabric around her hips and looking thoughtful.

"Should I have patted her on the head and told her that everything is going to be okay?" he demanded as Kasey pulled a strapless T-shirt over her bikini top.

He was annoyed to find himself holding his breath, waiting for her answer. He didn't want to mess this up and he didn't want Kasey to think that he had. Why was he concerned about her opinion? He didn't, generally, give a rat's ass about what people thought about him. But he respected Kasey...

"I think you did the right thing," Kasey said softly and his stomach unraveled an inch or two. "I'd far prefer that you hurt me with the truth rather than comfort me with a lie."

Aaron sent a glance to the empty house. "But she's so little..."

"Kids respect honesty, Aaron. You made progress with her by telling her the truth."

"Honesty is a big deal for me," Aaron said, looking into her lovely face.

"It's a big deal for me, too," Kasey replied, picking up the towel Savvie had left on the patio floor. When she straightened, Aaron caught the flash of deep-seated pain in her eyes, in the way her lips thinned, and wondered who'd lied to her and why. He opened his mouth to ask her but then remembered he had no right to go digging into her life. For eight months he'd managed—just barely—not to cross that line from business to personal, but since he'd kissed her in her bedroom, that line was out of focus and fuzzy.

Aaron picked up his T-shirt and pulled it over his head. "I'd better change."

Kasey folded the towels she was holding, paying the menial task much more attention than it deserved. "And I need to catch up on my day job." She turned away but Aaron caught her elbow and sighed at her soft skin, the scent of her perfume mingling with the chlorine smell of the pool. "Kase?"

Whiskey-honeyed eyes threatened to buckle his knees. "Yeah?"

He wanted to kiss her, to yank her to him, to plunder her sexy mouth and fill his hands with her plump breasts. He wanted to strip her out of her clothes and lay her down on that lounger and make love to her in the afternoon sun. Then wanted to take her into the pool to see if pool sex was as good as he remembered.

Aaron noticed the tremble in Kasey's fingers, the way her pulse fluttered in her neck. She'd let him. He knew this as well as he knew his own handwriting. It was a fantastic fantasy but it was a crap idea. "Nothing. I'd better go."

Kasey nodded, started to speak, but then gave the tiniest shake of her head, clamped her lips shut and headed into the house without saying another word.

Three

Kasey sent the email, leaned back in her chair and rolled her head from side to side, trying to ease the tension in her neck.

She glanced at her messy desk, relieved that she was finally caught up. The work didn't stop because Savannah needed her. The clients, and her boss, still demanded their pound of flesh and their pint of blood.

Kasey looked out the huge window, noticed that the sun was starting to drop, and eyed her watch. Six thirty? Aaron and Savannah should've been home ages ago.

Where had the last two hours gone? Kasey closed down her computer and picked up the phone on her desk. She'd call Aaron and ask where they were. Savannah needed to eat, have a bath and be in bed by eight. She was almost six, not sixteen...

Kasey started to dial his number before remembering that Aaron was Savvie's guardian and if he wanted to keep her up all night, he could. She was just the temporary nanny, she had no right to phone and harangue him about his parenting skills. Kasey dropped the phone back into its cradle. Aaron was, possibly, the most responsible man she knew. Savannah would be fine.

The adults in Savvie's life—Aaron and Megan— were fully functional.

Her own parents were young when they'd had her and had no idea how to parent responsibly or how to parent at all. She didn't remember much of her early childhood but her few memories didn't place her parents in the best light.

Apart from the constant moves and the ten schools in twelve years, she remembered falling asleep behind a couch, her stomach cramping because her parents were too drunk to feed her, waking up in a stranger's house because they had forgotten to take her home with them when they'd left a party. Bedtime was when she was tired, supper was always takeout, bathing was optional.

The summer holidays spent with her grandparents had been blissfully normal. There were rules and those rules had made her feel safe and cared for. There was healthy food, plenty of sunshine, lots of time to play. Her grandparents were two stable, hardworking people who respected the hell out of each other, loved each other even more, and she'd desperately craved what they'd had. Love, friendship, stability...a proper home. She'd thought Dale could give that to her, which showed how ridiculously moronic she could be on occasion and how skewed her judgment was.

Kasey stood and pushed her chair back, stretching her back to work out the kinks. Through the open window she heard the low purr of Aaron's SUV coming up the long driveway and her mouth curved up... They were home.

Leaving the office, she hurried down the stairs, walked into the informal sitting room and headed toward the back hallway, which was almost as impressive as the main entrance. Instead of pulling his big vehicle into the five-car garage, Aaron stopped a few meters from her. He cut the engine, the back door opened and Savannah all but tumbled out of the car, hair a mess and eyes blazing.

Oh, God, what happened? Had they found Jason? Kasey darted a look at Aaron, who was walking around the hood of the car, and he shook his head, silently telling her it wasn't what she thought. "Kasey! Kasey!" Savannah hurtled toward her, flung her arms around her waist and buried her face in Kasey's stomach.

Kasey bent over the little girl, stroking her hair and lifting her eyebrows at Aaron. "What's going on?" she asked as Savannah wrenched herself off her and streaked to the back of the SUV.

"Kasey, come see! Quick! Come look."

Oh, dear Lord, Kasey thought, jamming her hands

in the back pockets of her jeans. What had Aaron done? Whatever it was, it was earning big points with Savvie. Aaron tossed her a cheeky smile, opened the big back door of the SUV and turned around, a hairy ball of fur in his arms.

"His name is Kanga, Kasey, and he's a New-find-me," Savannah said, gripping the puppy's hairy face with both hands before kissing its nose. Kanga responded by licking Savvie's cheek.

"It's a Newfoundland puppy," Aaron corrected her, tucking the enormous puppy under his arm. He smiled at Kasey.

Kasey scratched the puppy behind his ears and lifted her eyebrows at Aaron. "When I said a dog, I meant a crossbreed from the pound."

"He is from the pound. Well, sort of. His mother's owner is facing financial difficulties. She asked the manager of the shelter to help her find a home." Aaron glanced down at Savannah, who still was nose to nose with the pup. "Savannah fell in love, what could I do?"

"Say no?" Kasey suggested sotto voce. "You do know that they are monstrous dogs, that they can reach one hundred twenty pounds and that they drool?"

Aaron's big, broad hand stroked Kanga's coal-black head. "She fell in love, Kase!"

Kasey's lips twitched. "Sucker. Good thing you have space and that you can afford the veterinary and food bill. He's going to cost a fortune, Aaron."

"They are."

Kasey sent him a puzzled look. "What?"

Aaron exchanged a conspiratorial look with Savannah and swung open the back door of the SUV. Another puppy, also a Newfoundland and even bigger than Kanga, but a rich, chocolate brown, sprawled across the cargo area. "Kanga and Roo came as a package deal, part of the reason why the shelter manager couldn't find homes for them."

The little girl leaned into the car and pushed her face into Roo's warm coat. When she lifted her head to look at Kasey, her eyes glistened with tears. "I love my puppies, Kasey." Pulling back, she turned around and hugged Aaron's hips. "Thank you, Uncle Aaron."

"My pleasure, kiddo." Aaron barely got the words out before Roo sat up and exploded to life. He barked once and barreled out of the vehicle, nearly mowing Savannah down in the process. Kanga wriggled and, because he was caught off guard, managed to slip from Aaron's grasp. Within ten seconds, two puppies the size of lion cubs and the dark-haired girl were streaking through the gardener's perfectly planted flower beds and across the manicured lawn.

Aaron placed his hands on his hips and watched Savannah fall to the grass, the puppies crawling over her, tugging her hair and licking her face.

"So, this is going to be fun," he said, sounding doubtful.

Kasey shook her head. "I have only one thing to say."

Aaron lifted an eyebrow. "Yeah?"

"I want a raise."

* * *

In the Royal Diner, Kasey looked at her watch, grateful that she had a little time to unwind before she needed to leave to collect Savannah from summer day camp. She relaxed against the back of the red faux-leather booth and looked out onto the busy road bisecting downtown Royal. It was a hive of activity; pickup trucks and sports cars were parked on either side of the road or were rolling down the wide boulevard. The residents of Royal ambled along clean sidewalks, lifting their hands in greeting and often stopping to chat. There was a sense of community here, Kasey realized, a small-town vibe she liked.

Amanda Battle, who Kasey knew to be the owner of the diner, stopped by her booth, holding a coffee-pot. "Can I give you a refill?"

Kasey returned her open, happy smile. "Thanks, but I'm fine. I'm—"

"Kasey Monroe, Aaron's whiz of an assistant, temporary nanny to Savvie," Amanda replied, resting her hand on her hip. She laughed at Kasey's surprise. "This is Royal, honey, where gossip is the town's favorite sport. You're from Houston and you're either a snob or heartbroken, because you don't socialize much. In fact, this is the first time I've seen you in here for months."

"Not a snob," Kasey said.

"Heartbroken?"

"I was, but I'm better now," Kasey replied and realized that it was true. She did feel better. Okay, so maybe with a broken marriage and a ruined friendship behind her, she wasn't living the idyllic, roses-and-champagne life she'd envisioned, but she was, temporarily, living in a fantastic house with a kid who thought she was pretty wonderful, two crazy dogs who kept her constantly entertained and her sin-fully sexy boss.

"Finally!"

Kasey heard the familiar voice and every cell in her body tensed. Her world tilted. Kasey blinked, once, then twice, dimly aware that Michelle's red lips were touching her cheek, that she was sliding onto the bench opposite her and tossing her bag on the table between them.

Kasey felt Amanda's hand on her shoulder, heard her soft command to breathe. She did as she was told and the world refocused. Kasey looked into Amanda's sympathetic face and held up her cup. "Suddenly, I need a refill."

"And I'll have—"

"She's not staying," Kasey interrupted Michelle's carefree chirp.

Amanda's eyes bounced from Kasey to Michelle and back again. One arched eyebrow lifted. "Do you want her gone?" Amanda asked. "My husband, Nate, is the sheriff and he can be here in two minutes."

It was tempting, so tempting, but she really didn't want to cause a scene. "I'll let you know."

"You do that, hon." Amanda frowned at Michelle. "You, behave."

Michelle pouted, resting her forearms on the table.

"Who does she think she is? She can't speak to me like that!"

Kasey matched her former friend's frown with one of her own. "What are you doing here, Michelle?"

Again, the pout. "You've never called me by my full name, it's always been Mish."

"That was before you slept with my husband."

"Are you still harping on that? God, it didn't mean anything! It was just sex! We were drunk and high."

"It meant something to me!" Kasey retorted. Why was this so difficult for her to understand?

"It was a mistake, Kase, I admit it." Michelle used one perfectly manicured finger to push her long blond fringe out of her eyes, then tapped the table with the fake nail of her index finger. "But I don't see sex the same way you do. Dale and I? We look at it differently."

Marginally interested in an explanation that made some sort of sense but damned if she'd ask her to elaborate, Kasey tipped her head to the side.

"Sex is a game, some fun, a passing fancy. It's an itch to scratch, a cool drink on a hot day. Add booze and drugs and it means even less."

Kasey heard the truth in Michelle's voice. She genuinely believed what she was saying but her lack of emotional intelligence was breathtaking. Had she always been this way? Had Kasey just been looking at her through rose-colored lenses?

Michelle's brown eyes met hers. "Can we get past this? I miss you so much."

"I miss you, too," Kasey quietly admitted. And

she did. Michelle, with her devil-may-care attitude to life, could always make her laugh.

The other woman's eyes flashed with hope. "So, does that mean we're good?"

Kasey shook her head, her eyes burning with tears she refused to allow to fall. "I don't know. I don't think so. Because no matter what your attitude toward sex is, to me, it's an expression of love and I loved Dale. Booze or not, as my best friend, he was forever and ever off-limits." She swallowed hard. "I need more time to work through this, so…give me some space, okay?"

Michelle gnawed on her bottom lip. "I'm thinking about moving here, to Royal. With you gone, there's not much left for me in Houston…"

Kasey's stomach sank to her shoes. "Please don't, Michelle. I need distance from you, from what happened."

"But I need to be here, so when you do forgive me, we can be like we were."

Sighing, Kasey stood, grabbed her tote bag and slung it over her shoulder. Their friendship would never be the same again. Even if she managed to forgive Michelle, this would always be between them. "I need time. I need space. If you love me at all, please respect that."

Kasey looked at Amanda, who was heading toward her with a fresh cup of coffee in her hand. Walking away from Michelle, she reached into the back pocket of her jeans and pulled out some crumpled bills.

Amanda darted a look at Michelle and took the

payment. "You should join our book club, we meet every couple of weeks."

Kasey felt touched at the offer. "I'd love to, but I don't have time to read at the moment."

Amanda laughed. "When I say book club, it's mostly just an excuse to ditch our men and drink wine. I'll let you know the next time we're getting together."

Kasey frowned, surprised at the generous offer. "Why me? You don't really know me."

Amanda darted a look at a sulky Michelle and raised her eyebrows. "Because, honey, you definitely need more options when it comes to friends."

"Kasey?"

She was driving Savannah home and lifted her eyes to look at Savvie in the rearview mirror, sighing at the worry she saw in the little girl's eyes.

"Yeah, sweetie?"

Savannah sucked her lower lip between her teeth. "The kids at camp are asking whether I'm still having my party."

"What party, Savvie?"

"In two sleeps I'm going to be six and Daddy said that I could have my birthday party before I go to school. He said I could have a Princess Pool Party on Saturday."

Kasey blew air into her cheeks, silently cursing. This was the first time she'd heard about the party and her first instinct was to say that she didn't think it could happen, not with all the drama of her dad being missing. Kasey looked in the mirror again and saw the glimmer of hope in Savannah's eyes. Stuff it, she thought. The kid was going through hell and, sure, she had a lot to do, but how hard would it be to organize a princess party?

"I think your dad would've wanted you to have that party, Savvie." Kasey grinned at the whoop of joy coming from the back seat. "Let's do it."

"Yay!" Savannah shouted.

Kasey heard excitement and happiness in her voice.

She started to make mental lists, but her mind kept drifting back to her conversation with Michelle and the drama that seemed to follow her friend around. She was so over it...

It was easier to think about Aaron, who, on so many levels, intrigued her. Initially she'd been attracted to his looks but she quickly realized that he was so much more than a pretty shell. Aaron was phenomenally smart and she enjoyed, and appreciated, his quick mind.

But she'd known smart, handsome men before and they'd never caused her knees to shake and her mouth to water. His brain and body combo was distracting but his big heart, his integrity and his flat out honesty made him so very difficult to resist.

It would've been so easy for Aaron to pressure her to continue sleeping with him after she took the job as his assistant; they lived in the same town and they'd had spectacular sex. It would've been easy to carry on their affair and, because she'd been so vulnerable, she might've welcomed the distraction of a hot affair.

That never happened. From the day she started work, she kept expecting Aaron to make a reference to that night and how incredible it had been but he'd kept his word and had never so much as hinted to what they'd done to and with each other. Looking back, she was so grateful he'd been so professional. She'd needed that time to heal, to come to terms with her failed marriage and Michelle's betrayal.

The other day, when she kissed him, he'd been the one to slam on the brakes, to back off. He was her boss and to Aaron, kissing her was, at best, inappropriate. Kasey knew, on an instinctive level, that she could strip naked in front of Aaron, crawl all over him and be on the point of no return but if she changed her mind, said no, Aaron would back off.

And the next day he'd treat her with the same respect he'd always afforded her.

She trusted Aaron's honor and was completely convinced that she was, would always be, in control of their blazing attraction and that her job would never be used as a weapon against her.

She also knew that she really, really wanted to sleep with him again.

That night they spent together had been one of the most positive, life-affirming, healing experiences of her life. As he touched her, with reverence and care, she'd felt some of the fissures in her heart heal, her confidence seep back. There was something amazing about having a strong, masculine man worshipping her body that filled a woman with a sense of power and control. And knowing that Aaron enjoyed her touch as much as she did made her feel…what?

Potent, blissful, buoyant?

All of those, but Aaron also made her feel like herself, more like herself than she'd felt for a long time, possibly forever. When she was around him, she felt like the best version she could be…

But, despite the way he made her feel, she couldn't afford to become hooked on anyone again.

With a headache threatening to split her head in two, Kasey pulled into her designated spot in the garage, in between the very expensive Vanquish and Aaron's new SUV and wished that she could stay in the car, where it was quiet and cool. But Savannah needed a snack and she still had research to do for Aaron. And a party to plan.

She had to get her head on straight, to stop thinking about Aaron and the way he made her feel. She trusted him to not allow sex to influence her working life, she trusted him with her body, but it was smarter and safer to leave the situation as it was, to not rock the boat by suggesting that they explore the bubbling, roiling crazy chemistry between them…

Dale and Michelle had taught her that the only person she could fully trust, rely on, was herself. It was always better to keep her heart out of the firing line.

Kasey heard Savvie exit the car and closed her eyes. She desperately needed to get out of her head, to stop, for a few minutes, thinking and obsessing and remembering. Dale, Michelle, Aaron…all three of them, to some degree, frustrated and confused her. She needed to run off her frustration and as soon as she could, she'd put on her trainers, pull up her hair and hit the road. And if she shed a tear or two while she ran, nobody would know.

Kasey heard Savannah greet Kanga and Roo and she was off and running with her favorite friends. Walking around the car, she slung Savannah's backpack over her shoulder, picked up the bag of groceries and her bag, nudging the door shut with her knee. She went into the house through the garage door and into the utility room. Kasey frowned at the pile of dry laundry in the basket, now wrinkled and creased.

Continuing on into the kitchen, she placed the sack of groceries on the counter and Savannah's backpack over the arm of a dining chair. She wrinkled her nose when she saw a stack of dirty dishes in the sink. Aaron's housekeeper had taken a fall two days ago and was out of commission with a torn hamstring. It was rapidly becoming clear to Kasey that the two other occupants in the house assumed that the fairies—her—would magically make the mess disappear.

Taking a deep, calming breath, she glanced across the open-plan space, saw that Savannah had found the TV remote and was watching her favorite kids program, the puppies turning her into a Savannah sandwich. A glass holding an inch of juice stood on the side table, along with a side plate holding the skin of an orange. A sheaf of papers was on the floor and, even from a distance, Kasey could see that it was the twenty-page report she'd burned the midnight oil to compile for Aaron. And, on one of the pages, was that a paw print?

Seriously?

Kasey looked around and saw that the huge doors leading onto the outdoor area were open and that one of her trainers lay just outside the door. Temper bubbling, she hurried across the room and onto the patio, cursing when she saw that the shoe was not only ripped to shreds but soaking wet with puppy drool. Puppy drool and something yellow... God, they'd eaten her shoe and then peed on it!

No trainers, which meant no running until she managed to replace them.

"Kasey!"

She turned around slowly and saw Aaron walking into the room, his state-of-the-art tablet in his hand, his mouth taut with displeasure. With a final look at her mangled shoe—dammit!—she stepped into the house and looked at her grumpy but still sexy boss.

"Have you managed to source any information yet on that wind turbine company?" he demanded.

Aaron had given her the assignment as she was walking out of the door to collect Savvie, an hour earlier. She'd spent twenty minutes at the Royal Diner, picked Savannah up and then hit the grocery store to stock up on kitchen essentials. She'd come home and found the house a mess and her trainers in shreds. When would she have had the time?

It took all she had not to snap. "No, I haven't."

"I need that information, Kasey. The company is

courting a few investors and I don't want to miss out on this opportunity because you can't do your job."

She knew that she should cut Aaron some slack. That he was desperately worried about his brother. That he wasn't sleeping. That he was struggling with the crazy reality that was now his life…

But with a now-throbbing headache, she was feeling less than tolerant. Kasey placed her hands on her hips and tossed him an irate look. "You're kidding me, right?"

Aaron finally looked up from his screen to glance at her. "I need that information, Kasey. Like, in the next thirty minutes."

"Then go online and get it yourself," Kasey told him, anger roiling through her.

Aaron's eyes turned wintry. "Excuse me? Do you or do you not work for me?"

Kasey saw that Savannah was kneeling on the couch, looking at them with worried eyes. They couldn't fight in front of her, so Kasey told her to take Kanga and Roo outside to play ball. Savannah scrambled off the sofa, ran past the adults and out onto the patio.

"What is your problem?" Aaron asked, placing his tablet on the dining table before opening the fridge to pull out a bottle of water. He cracked the top and took a long swallow while Kasey tried to find the most diplomatic way to tell him that he was being an ass.

Nope, nothing. "You're an ass."

Aaron's thick eyebrows lifted.

"A demanding, selfish, annoying ass." Kasey

pushed the words out between her lips. So much for diplomacy.

"Have you even noticed that the housekeeper isn't here? Clean laundry scrunched up in the basket, dirty dishes in the sink." Kasey pointed to her report on the floor. "I only got to bed at around one this morning because I was up compiling that report, which I find strewn on the floor covered in paw prints. The puppies have peed under the dining table and God knows where else! I am running myself ragged trying to keep Savannah busy. I am doing my job, Aaron, but which one comes first? Savannah or research? Housekeeper or puppy minder? I also now have to plan Savannah's party for Saturday!"

"What party?"

"Her birthday party!"

Aaron winced, guilt flooding his features. "Dammit, I'd forgotten that it was her birthday soon. Maybe we should—"

Oh hell, no. They were not canceling! "She's having a party," Kasey said, sounding stubborn. "A Princess Pool Party, so don't argue."

"Okay but—"

Kasey, feeling overwhelmed, glanced around the room and her temper spiked again. "And those monsters you call dogs ate, and peed on, my favorite trainers!" she shouted. "All I wanted, Aaron—all that was keeping me going today, was the idea of getting out of this place, just for an hour, to run. To not think! Now I can't even do that!"

Kasey didn't realize that tears were running down

her face until Aaron's thumb wiped the moisture away. "Ah, honey."

Still seething, Kasey smacked her hands against his chest, feeling like she was a pressure cooker about to blow. She was about to blast him but she made the mistake of looking into his eyes, at that sexy, masculine mouth descending toward hers. This wasn't the time for kissing. She needed to tell him that she couldn't do this, that she wasn't coping.

Then Aaron's lips claimed hers and the world shifted, tumbled off its axis.

The thought occurred to her that she should push him away—she was mad, dammit!—but Aaron was kissing her, his lips moving across hers, his tongue coaxing her to play, and the only thing she could think of to do was to wind her arms around his neck and press her breasts into his chest. Her lips parted and then Aaron took the kiss deeper, wilder, hotter. Kasey could feel that he wanted her, it was in the sin-with-me strokes of his tongue, the big hand cupping her butt cheek, the massive erection pressed into her stomach.

If she couldn't run, then sex would be an equally good way to burn off her frustration. It was just sex, Kasey told herself, deliberately ignoring her earlier sex and heart argument. People did it all the time. And Aaron was particularly skilled. She ran her hands down his broad back, pulled his cotton shirt up and slid her hand down the hot skin of his lower back. A bolt of lust shot straight to that hot place between her legs as she dipped her fingers beneath the band of his boxers. She wanted him, she wanted *this*, so much. She wanted to forget about past betrayals, sad little girls and missing brothers. She wanted to ignore the dirty dishes and the laundry and puppy pee. She wanted to step out of her life and feel, be the object of this big, sexy man's undivided attention.

Aaron pulled his mouth off hers and Kasey moaned her disappointment. She reached up to carry on kissing him, missed his mouth and kissed his cheek. Kasey felt his hands on her hips and then realized that he was lifting her...

Away from him.

Wha-at?

Again?

Not content to be a selfish ass around the house, he was also rejecting her. Kasey wondered if this day could get any worse, before quickly reminding the universe that her statement wasn't a challenge. She glared at Aaron, who was rubbing the back of his neck, looking uncomfortable.

"Savvie's around and the kid has been traumatized enough without seeing us getting hot and heavy."

Kasey looked out into the garden, saw that Savannah and the puppies were under the live oaks at the bottom of the property. The little girl wasn't paying them the smallest bit of attention. Kasey turned her attention back to Aaron and frowned when he wouldn't look at her. Had he just kissed her to distract her from her rant? Was the kiss just a way to allow him to dodge the issue? Dale had used the exact same tactic all the time...all over her like a rash whenever they started to fight.

God, she was such an idiot. Kasey wanted to blast Aaron, but then she remembered that he was her boss, that she liked her job and, mostly, liked him. She'd agreed to be Savannah's nanny and, when she was feeling a little more rational, she'd tackle him about who was responsible for keeping the house from becoming a pigsty. But not right now. She needed to calm down, wash her face and head into the office to do some research on wind turbines. Work would help steady her and get them back on an even keel.

She needed to steady the ship.

"I want you, Kase," Aaron said, his voice tight. "Don't doubt that."

Even without his words Kasey knew that to be the truth. She saw it in the way his eyes connected with hers, the way he seemed to look into her soul. A muscle in his cheek jumped as if he were trying not to yank her to him and take her hard and fast. She didn't even need to drop her eyes to know that he was rock hard.

Don't, Kasey. Steady the ship, focus...do your job.

"Can you watch Savannah while I do my real job?" Kasey quietly asked, lifting her chin. If she had to work twenty hours a day, Aaron would never again accuse her of goofing off.

Aaron nodded. "Sure."

Kasey expressed her thanks, picked up her bag and started to walk out of the room. When Aaron called her name, she sighed. What now?

"In my desk drawer are some extra-strength aspirin. Take a couple. We'll talk when you're done."

"I'll have that report ready for you soon." She clipped the words out.

"Kasey—"

She didn't bother to stop but just walked away from him and hurried up the stairs.

Four

Well, hell.

Aaron watched Kasey walk out of the room, trying not to be distracted by the elegant sway of her hips and the fluidity of her long-legged stride. He started to follow her, realized what he was doing and slammed on brakes, attempting to push the idea of taking Kasey up against the wall or on the stairs out of his mind. Pulling away from her had been the hardest thing he'd ever done and, talking about hard, he needed a series of cold showers to settle the hell down.

Or sex. Sex with Kasey would take care of that problem. He couldn't ever remember wanting a woman this much.

She was driving him to the edge of lunacy.

Aaron gripped the bridge of his nose, cursing himself. He shouldn't have kissed her, but the combination of fire and pain in her eyes had aroused his protective streak and in that moment he'd wanted to kick anyone and anything that caused her even a smidgen of worry.

Even if it was his own ass he had to kick.

Exhaling roughly, he placed his hands on the kitchen counter, straightened his arms and looked around his house. Yeah, those were his dirty dishes on the coffee table. He'd meant to take care of them but he'd been distracted by an email and then a phone call.

Mrs. B had been injured and it had never crossed his mind as to who was keeping his palatial home clean, who was keeping him and Savannah organized. He'd been so caught up in his life, trying to keep his business on track and his niece happy—his concern for Jason a constant ache in the back of his mind— that he'd ignored the practical aspects of running a household. Or, worse, it had been easy to allow Kasey to pick up the slack.

He was, officially, a jerk. Kasey was working long hours and he'd been unreasonable with his demands and disrespectful of her work. Annoyed with himself, Aaron walked over to the sitting area and picked her report up from the floor. He'd been in the process of reading it when the puppies had jumped him and it had fallen to the floor, their paws landing on it. He smoothed the creases and placed the papers under his tablet. After straightening the cushions on the sofas, he picked up his dirty dishes, turned the TV off and headed back to the kitchen.

He was, mostly, a modern guy and believed that guys could do housework and girls could handle guns. Just because Kasey was acting as Savvie's nanny, that didn't mean she needed to cook and clean, as well. He should've been on top of this. He shouldn't have assumed that she would just take care of his niece and, by extension, him.

Besides, that wasn't the way he wanted her to take care of him. He wanted to feel the strands of her hair brush his stomach as she went down on him, her warm mouth wrapped around him. He'd allow her to build him up to a certain point before lifting her so that she straddled his hips, driving up and into her, her cries of pleasure slowing him down...

Yeah, thinking about sex is so helpful, Phillips. God, you are so screwed. Metaphorically.

Get your mind out of the bedroom and back on track!

To make life easier for Kasey, her role had to be more clearly defined and it was up to him to make that happen. And that meant that he had to get his raging attraction to her under control. No more kissing, no more lying awake, feeling guilty for fantasizing about having Kasey in his bed, in a number of explicit and erotic positions. He was unfocused; he should be worrying about Jason's welfare. And Savannah's. His sister, Megan's...

Aaron watched as Savannah walked to the house, a puppy on each side of her, one of her hands on each head. If Jason was dead—and with every day that passed that was becoming more likely—how was he going to cope with raising his niece on his own?

Kasey's help was temporary; he couldn't rely on her on a long-term basis. He'd have to hire a nanny, but the thought of a stranger moving into his house, replacing Kasey, who would leave his home and go back to her pretty little cottage in Royal, made his stomach churn. He liked seeing her face in the morning, walking down the stairs into the kitchen, seeing both his girls eating breakfast...

God, she wasn't *his* girl, she was his assistant. Why did these crazy images of a happily-ever-after keep popping into his head?

Savannah wasn't his daughter, Kasey was never going to be a permanent part of his personal life, and he was just making life that much harder for himself. Kate taught him that romantic dreams were nightmares in disguise, that loyalty was a fickle concept to most and that few people could be trusted.

His parents' death and Jason's disappearance reminded him that everybody he loved had a nasty habit of disappearing on him. So it was imperative that he keep his distance from Kasey. And that also meant keeping his hands off her. Not that Kasey would want to come anywhere near him anytime soon since he was a selfish jerk who only thought about himself.

For some reason, one Aaron didn't want to investigate, the notion of Kasey thinking badly of him left a sour taste in his mouth. And he had an idea of how to get rid of it.

* * *

Kasey sent a copy of her report to Aaron's email address and printed a hard copy, which she placed on his desk. Work, as it had for the last eight months, settled her emotions and she felt back in control. She wished she could sneak off to her room, exhaustion and embarrassment were a toxic combination, but she'd been upstairs for ninety minutes and she had a second job to do: a child to look after.

Ten more days until she could leave and go back to her cottage and her normal, albeit boring life, Kasey thought. Could she do it? Of course she could... Jeez, people survived not eating for ten days, she could cope with her attraction to her sexy but presently annoying boss and her fondness for a fairy child.

After brushing her hair and washing her face and hands, Kasey swiped on a layer of lip gloss and headed downstairs, thinking about what she could make for dinner. She wasn't keen on takeout—she'd had too much as a child—but the thought of whipping up something nutritious and filling made her want to whimper.

Stir fry? A chicken salad?

Kasey was taking a mental inventory of the fridge when she walked into the informal living area where they spent most of their time. Nothing came to mind and she was too tired to be creative.

But, since Savannah was setting the table, it had to be assumed that Aaron and Savvie were expecting food. She was going to have to cave and order takeout.

Kasey glanced to her right and saw the puppies

lying by the door, both of them chewing on either end of a yellow, rubber chicken. The puddle they'd made earlier had been wiped away and her shoe was gone.

The room looked immaculate.

Aaron, she thought on an appreciative sigh. As if her thoughts had conjured him, he walked out of the utility room, wiping his hands on a kitchen towel. Kasey, feeling embarrassed, jammed her hands into the back pockets of her khaki capris. "Your report is on your desk. I also sent it to your email address."

"I saw that," Aaron replied, opening a cupboard and removing two large wineglasses. Gesturing to an icy bottle of white wine, he lifted his eyebrows in a can-I-pour-you-a-glass gesture. Kasey nodded and walked over to the kitchen counter to take possession of the glass of deliciousness.

"Savvie, shower time," Aaron said. "Can you manage by yourself or do you need some help?"

Savannah rolled her eyes. "Of course I can manage, I'm practically six, Uncle Aaron."

His lips twitched. "Okay, kiddo. Well, then, run upstairs while I have a chat with Kasey."

"Your pj's are under your pillow," Kasey told her. "Yell if you need me."

Savannah nodded, flashed Kasey a small smile and ran past them, Kanga and Roo at her heels. "No dogs in the shower, Savvie!" she called out, not wanting to deal with the mess one girl and two monsters could make in the bathroom.

"Aw…" Savannah groaned.

When Kasey heard her feet on the wooden stairs, she looked at Aaron. "I owe you an apology for earlier."

Aaron picked up their glasses and walked around the counter. "Let's take this outside, it's a nice night."

Kasey followed him onto the patio and sank into one of the comfortable wicker chairs. Aaron, still in his black cargo shorts and white T-shirt, kicked off his flip-flops and placed his big feet on the square coffee table.

He sipped his wine and looked over his garden before those mesmerizing eyes met hers. "I'm the one who owes you an apology, Kase. Mrs. B spoils me and I'm used to being waited on." He sighed. "I'm sorry. As you so eloquently pointed out, I've been a pain in the ass."

He had been, but she also knew there were extenuating circumstances. Jason's disappearance had to be killing him. She wanted to say something encouraging, to tell him that Jason would be walking through that door soon, back into their lives. But they would be empty words. Jason would've been here a long time ago if he wasn't hurt. Or worse. "Thanks for cleaning up."

"I also shoved the laundry back into the dryer. Packed the dishwasher."

Kasey smiled at him. "Thank you. If you tell me that you've thought about a plan for supper, I just might kiss you."

The words left her mouth and she blushed when Aaron sent her a wicked smile. "Since dinner is in the oven and a salad is made, I'll take you up on that offer."

Kasey grinned. "You made dinner? Awesome! What is it?"

"Lasagna from the Royal Diner," Aaron replied. "One of Amanda's waitstaff delivered a tray while you were upstairs. Oh, and I've arranged with Amanda to deliver a cooked meal every day until Mrs. B gets back."

Now Kasey felt guilty. "I just had a bad day today, you didn't have to do that."

"Cooking was never the deal and you have enough on your plate," Aaron conceded, his expression thoughtful. "Amanda asked after you. She said that you met someone at the diner, that you looked upset when you left the restaurant. Whose butt do I need to go kick?"

His tone was mild but Kasey could see the concern on his face and knew that if she said the word, Aaron would jump in and fight this battle for her. Being strong and independent, and not prepared to rely on a man again, she'd never let that happen, but it was a nice thought. "Just someone from my past."

Aaron dropped his feet, placed his wineglass on the coffee table and leaned forward, determination all over his handsome face. "It's obvious to me that the confrontation was a contributing factor to your meltdown this afternoon. Tell me what happened, Kasey."

Kasey held her wineglass to her chest, undecided. Then he added a low-pitched "Please," and the words started rolling off her tongue.

"I saw Michelle at the diner. I've known her since I was ten. She used to be my best, closest friend."

"What did she do?"

Kasey sipped her wine before resting the glass on her knee. "She slept with my ex-husband. She says it was a drunken mistake. That it meant nothing." She released a pent-up breath. "She thinks I should forgive her, that what they had was just sex, that there weren't any emotions involved."

"But yours were." Aaron reached across the table, took her glass from her hand and put it on the table between them. It was only then that she realized her hand was shaking.

"You get that?" Kasey asked.

"Sure, I get that. It doesn't matter how they view sex. Whether it meant anything or not, fidelity, loyalty and monogamy mean something to you, so they should've respected that."

"Michelle doesn't understand that. She wants me to go back to how we were before."

"Can you see yourself doing that?"

Kasey thought about it for a minute. "A part of me does. I miss her, Aaron, I miss having someone to talk to, someone I believe in and who believes in me. Before I walked in on them, I really believed that Michelle was the one person I could go to if I had a dead body in the trunk, knowing that she'd grab a shovel. Without her, I feel lost. But so betrayed."

Aaron's big hand enveloped his glass. "And your ex? Is he wanting to come back into your life, as well?"

Kasey pulled a face. "There have been some calls, which I'm ignoring." Kasey shrugged her shoulders.

"I was stupid. I thought he could give me the family and the stability I wanted. None of it makes sense to me."

Aaron's perceptive look sliced though her. "Do you want it to? Do you need to understand before you can move on?"

Kasey rubbed her hands up and down her arms. "I don't think I want to move on, not in the way I think you mean. I'm really not interested in a relationship, in commitment. My marriage and divorce stripped fifty layers off me and it's an experience I'd prefer not to repeat."

"So us sleeping together really was purely sexual?"

She blushed, remembering how erotic their night had been. "Dale was the last person I'd slept with before you. I didn't want all my memories of sex being of him." Kasey looked down before flashing him a quick smile. "Thanks to you, I know that sex isn't insipid or boring."

Aaron just stared at her for a long time before shaking his head. "Seriously, some guys would be better off being neutered."

"No argument from me," Kasey replied, chuckling wryly. She swallowed some wine, enjoying the hot night, the deepening sky and Aaron's company. This was what she'd wanted with Dale—company at the end of a long day, unwavering support and a few laughs. Was that really so much to ask?

Aaron's big hand covered hers, sending that intense tingle up her arm, jerking her back to the present. "If you want to, we could talk to Nate—"

"Who?"

"Nate Battle, the sheriff? He's Amanda's husband and, if he sees your friend hanging around, he could warn her off. Or threaten her with a restraining order."

Kasey knew that he was just being Aaron, innately protective, intensely loyal. Within five minutes of starting to work for Aaron she'd realized it was dangerous to mess with her boss's family, his friends or his employees. He gathered everybody under his wing and would go to war for those he loved. Not that he loved her—of course he didn't—but she was an essential cog in his professional wheel. Since she was also Savvie's primary caregiver at the moment, she kept his personal life running smoothly, as well.

Kasey wondered what being loved by a man like Aaron would be like. And why hadn't any of the Royal females, Houston bachelorettes—hell, any single women in the state—bagged him? Like astrophysics and artificial intelligence, she simply could not comprehend why he was still single.

He was so damn sexy…

Kasey held Aaron's gaze and the moisture in her mouth disappeared as desire replaced concern on his face, his thumb stroking the inside of her wrist in a slow, sure, delicious slide. It took everything she had not to lean forward, to place her lips on his. Her fast heartbeat and flushed skin, the heat she felt between her legs and her jittery heart were just her libido telling her that she was a relatively young woman who had needs. Sexual needs. And pleasuring herself just wasn't cutting it anymore.

Sometimes the only thing that satisfied was a ripped masculine body and big hands, a sexy mouth and a long, smooth—

"Kasey!"

Thin arms wrapped around her neck and she could smell strawberries, meaning that Savannah had found, and used, her bodywash. Thoughts of Aaron's wonderful body and how he could satisfy her were banished when Savannah buried her face in Kasey's neck. Caught off guard by this open display of affection, she turned in her seat and pulled the little girl onto her lap. "You okay, cupcake?"

Savannah turned those vibrant green eyes on hers—her father's eyes, Aaron's eyes—and blinked slowly. "Uncle Aaron said that you are feeling a little sad and that we need to love you a little more than usual."

Kasey's heart bumped and her gaze flew to Aaron's face, but he'd slid down his chair, his head resting on the back, and his eyes were closed.

"I was a little cross earlier, Savvie, but I'm fine now," she told her.

"How fine?" Savannah demanded, and Kasey saw the concern in her eyes. This little girl didn't need to worry about her, as well.

"Fine fine." Wanting to distract her, Kasey danced her fingers up her ribs and Savannah giggled.

"No-oo, I'm ticklish. And if you don't stop tickling me, you won't get your present."

Kasey's hands immediately stilled. "Present?" She loved presents, probably because there had been so few as a kid.

"Where did'ja put it, Uncle Aaron?"

He cracked one eye open, dropped his hand and pulled a shoebox from beneath his seat. It wasn't wrapped, so Kasey presumed that Savannah made something at school and Aaron found her a shoebox to house the gift. She looked at the designer brand of running shoes and sighed. One day, maybe, she might be able to afford a pair of these top-flight running shoes. Kasey scowled at the puppies, thinking since hers were in shreds, any trainers would be an improvement.

Savannah took the box from Aaron and pushed it against Kasey's chest. "Open it."

It was probably a drawing or a papier-mâché sculpture or something made from Play-Doh, Kasey told herself. No matter what it was, she had to be excited purely because Savannah was wriggling around, beside herself with anticipation.

Kasey lifted the box and shook it, surprised at how heavy it was. Savannah tried to tug the box out of her hands, impatient. "I'll do it! You're too slow."

Aaron sat up and placed a gentle hand on Savannah's small shoulder. "It's Kasey's present, Savvie, remember? To tell her that we'll do better?"

A tiny frown appeared between Kasey's eyebrows. It sounded like Aaron had been involved in this present, like it might have even been his idea. Her eyes slammed into his and the corners of his mouth tipped up in that sexy half smile that made her want to crush her mouth against his.

"I think you should open it before Savannah loses her mind," Aaron suggested, laughter coating his words.

Kasey placed the box on Savannah's thighs, lifted the lid and gasped at the multicolored trainers nestling in thin white paper. They were too small for Aaron's huge feet and too big for Savannah's and—Kasey peered at the shoe size—exactly right for her. She let out an undignified "Whoop!" before lifting one of the shoes from the box. It was a trail shoe, the one she'd wanted forever, in her size, and the color was perfect.

It had been two hours since she'd lost her sense of humor and in that time, Aaron had ordered supper, cleaned and tidied up, bought and had delivered a pair of running shoes? Her eyes slammed into his. "How? Why?"

Aaron smiled. "The why is easy—one or both of the demented duo ate your shoe and the shoes needed to be replaced. The how was as easy. I called the sports shop in Royal, spoke to the manager, and the kid who delivered the food from the Royal Diner picked up the shoes, as well."

Kasey cradled the box and the little girl to her chest, looking over Savannah's head to the man who kept surprising her. She didn't know what to say but... "Thank you. You didn't need to."

"I really did," Aaron assured her as he stood.

Kasey looked up at him, six foot plus of pure gorgeousness. With that wide chest, big arms, narrow hips, those long, long legs, he was the complete package. But more than that, he was also chivalrous. And kind.

And, dammit, while resisting his body had been torture, stopping herself from wanting to inch closer to him emotionally was, she was sure, going to be the death of her.

Since tomorrow was Saturday, Savvie had begged to stay up late.

Instead of heading up to his office to catch up on some work or to cruise the web for any sign of his brother, Aaron had stayed downstairs and spent ninety minutes watching an animated movie about cars and planes.

A quarter of the way through the movie, Savvie had crawled between them and fallen asleep, her head on Kasey's thigh and her legs sprawled over his. When he glanced over ten minutes later, Kasey was also asleep, her thick eyelashes dark against her creamy skin. Thinking they looked comfortable enough, he let them sleep, knowing that if Jason or Will knew he was willingly watching an animated movie, they'd take away his man card.

Well, maybe Jason wouldn't, but his other friend would. Sleeping girls, ice cream and animated movies were not a normal part of his life.

But hell, nothing was normal anymore. He couldn't keep his hands off his employee…he was the owner of two hyperactive puppies…Savannah was a little happier but…

Jason was still missing.

The credits started to roll over the huge flat-screen on the wall opposite them as Aaron picked his phone off the side table next to him. He swiped his thumb across the screen to wake the device. He had emails, but when he opened the program, they were all work-related. There was nothing from Will or Cole.

Aaron tapped out a quick message to Cole and cc'd Will.

There must be something we can do. Some lead we aren't pursuing.

Will replied first.

Richard Lowell has, literally, taken over my life. Jason is one of my best friends. Do you honestly believe that we aren't doing everything possible to find them both and get some answers?

Aaron read the message and tapped the face of the phone against his forehead. When Will put it like that…

But Jason was his family, his blood. And he deeply resented the fact that he wasn't part of the search, that he was relegated to the sidelines. He wasn't a sit-on-his-haunches type of guy: when he went after something, he threw his entire self into it. He'd dropped out of college, knowing he would be okay, convinced that he was making the right decision. Sometimes he regretted not having that piece of paper but it certainly hadn't affected his earning ability. It had been so much more important to his folks than it had been to him, hence their overreaction when he'd told them he was quitting.

He'd turned to Kate for comfort and she'd given him all the sex he'd wanted—he'd been young and stupid and assumed that love and sex were the same thing—while plotting how best to shove the knife into his back. He glanced over at Kasey, thinking they were a matched pair; they'd both been royally screwed by people who'd said they loved them.

Aaron gently bent Savvie's legs back so that he could stand. He turned to face his two sleeping beauties. A tiny frown puckered Kasey's brow and he rubbed the side of his thumb between her eyebrows, wondering what she was dreaming about. Her useless ex and her devious friend? Kasey had thought he'd been joking when he'd offered to kick someone's ass earlier, but he hadn't been. He'd gladly rain a world of hurt down on Kasey's ex-husband and ex–best friend.

Aaron lowered his hand to cup Kasey's cheek.

Keep it tidy, Phillips, she's not asked for your help, nor your protection. She would not appreciate, nor does she need, your interference. She's strong and independent.

Aaron smiled despite himself. She was also stubborn and had a temper that made all his blood race south.

Don't go there, Phillips. Not if you want to keep your sanity.

He bent down, scooped Savvie up and cradled her

against his chest. She sighed, turning into him, and Aaron felt his heart contract when she nuzzled closer and then seemed to fall into an even deeper sleep.

A wave of emotion passed over him and he rested his lips in her hair as he walked her across the room toward the stairs that led to the upper floor. He'd been the cause of her grandparents' death and he couldn't find her father, but he'd be damned if he'd fail Savannah; she would have the best he could give her.

Unfortunately, Aaron wasn't sure that was enough.

Five

Aaron's footsteps descending the wooden stairs woke Kasey up. Keeping her eyes half-closed, she watched him walk past her on his way to the patio, then heard the click of puppy nails on the tiled floor.

"Outside, you idiots!" Aaron hissed.

Kasey opened her eyes fully and got an eyeful of Kanga's curly face before his warm and very wet tongue slurped her cheek, just missing the side of her mouth. Aaron grabbed hold of his collar and yanked him away as Kasey sat up and wiped the back of her hand across her face. *Eww*. Slobby kisses and puppy breath. What a way to wake up.

Cursing, Aaron clapped his hands, pointed to the door and both the puppies hurtled that way, mistakenly thinking it was playtime.

Kasey looked at the black screen of the TV and then at her watch. "How long have I been asleep?" she asked, trying to swallow her yawn.

"For most of the movie," Aaron replied. Standing by the folding back doors leading to the entertainment area, he jerked his chin. "Savvie is soundly asleep, so come for a walk with me."

Kasey bit the corner of her lip, thinking a smarter move would be to mosey on up the stairs and into the guest bedroom. Alone.

But suddenly she wasn't tired and, after months of a mostly solitary existence, the last thing she wanted was to be alone. She wanted to take a night walk with Aaron, to look up at the stars, to feel the night air on her skin. She wanted to inhale the smell of newly cut grass, and roses…and, if she was lucky, occasionally get a whiff of Aaron's unique scent. That combination of deodorant and cologne and soap that always made her knees liquefy.

She wanted *him*…

Releasing a deep, enervating breath, Kasey pulled on her sandals and walked past Aaron, her eyes bouncing across the dark grass to look for the hell-on-wheels puppies. "I can't see them," she muttered, her eyes slowly adjusting to the darkness beyond the entertainment area and the pool.

"They've bolted toward the live oak and the pond."

"Why didn't you put lights in the garden?" Kasey asked as they began to stroll down the path that snaked through his parklike estate.

"Because I like walking in the dark," Aaron said, placing a hand on her back.

Kasey felt Aaron's hand cover hers, and his fingers slid between hers. Her shoulder brushed his and Kasey resisted the urge to lay her head on his shoulder as they walked. Heat, want and need flowed through her, making her nipples tingle, her mouth dry and her core ache. This much temptation was dangerous. If she made a move, and she'd have to because Aaron's integrity wouldn't allow him to, would he reject her again? Could she stand it? She didn't think so.

Kasey tried to tug her hand away. "I don't want you to trip," Aaron said, keeping a firm grip on her hand.

Kasey left her hand in his, knowing she wasn't going to fall and thinking that Aaron knew that, too. Maybe he, like her, needed the physical connection as much as she did. Besides, how long had it been since she'd walked hand in hand with a man late at night? Too long, Kasey decided. Definitely long before Dale—

She wasn't going to think of Dale tonight, Kasey told herself. Or Michelle. She just wanted to hold Aaron's hand and stroll with him in the moonlight.

They walked on in silence, reaching the wood bench under the live oak that shaded a koi pond. Kasey looked down into the dark, still water but couldn't see any fish moving. "Are they asleep?"

"The fish?" Aaron asked, humor lacing his voice.

"Yes, the fish."

"I remember the landscape designer saying something about them hanging out on the bottom of the pond at night. They might be sleeping or they could be playing poker…who knows?"

Kasey grinned and bumped her shoulder into his. "Ha, ha."

Roo, not understanding the concept of said creatures needing their sleep, ran down the bank and belly flopped into the pond. Kanga followed two seconds later. Aaron yanked Kasey back to avoid the splash of water, his low laugh rumbling over her.

Kasey looked up at him and thought that he looked ten years younger, and, for a brief moment, that he looked like he didn't have a care in the world. She desperately wanted to keep him laughing. "What did the fish say when it hit a concrete wall?" Before he could answer she dropped the punchline. "Dam."

Aaron's lips twitched and, without missing a beat, he lobbied his own back. "When you have any really good fish jokes, let minnow."

"Not bad, cod do better," Kasey quipped.

Aaron wrapped his arm around her waist, pulling her close, and she felt laughter rumbling through him.

Kasey tipped her head up in a silent challenge but he shook his head, looking rueful. "I've got nothing."

"Lightweight," Kasey murmured, her hands on his biceps. "I have about a million stupid jokes."

"Save them for later, sweetheart. Right now I have other plans for that mouth," Aaron murmured. As she expected him to, he hesitated before asking. "Are you okay with that?"

Again, his integrity, his need to do right by her, took her breath away. She wanted to tell him how much she appreciated his offer, him, but the words stuck in her throat.

Unable to speak, she simply nodded.

Still feeling a little light-headed from seeing her normally oh-so-serious boss cracking up at her childish jokes, Kasey felt her knees buckle when he pulled her stomach into his hips and she felt the evidence of his desire. His right hand palmed her butt cheek, and Kasey sucked in a deep breath, lust scorching her nerve endings. Then Aaron's mouth plundered hers, taking her mouth in a kiss that was all about desire, about the need to possess, to conquer, to brand. A part of her—that spirited, independent part that rebelled at losing control—wanted to pull back, but the rest of her, the 90 percent that was totally turned on, slapped that thought away. She was a woman being kissed by a man who knew how to do it properly and, damn, she was going to enjoy it.

Needing more, needing to get closer, Kasey looped her arms around Aaron's neck and boosted herself up his body, her legs winding around his waist. He held her easily and, while his mouth devoured hers, she reveled in the feel of his shaft rubbing her core.

Aaron slid his tongue past her lips and she sighed into his mouth: he tasted like heaven, better than chocolate, smoother than wine. Of heat and spice and sex…

And then his mouth left hers as he pulled back, lifting one hand to tug her shirt out of her pants, to pull it up her body to reveal the lacy cup of her bra. Kasey looked down, saw her nipple trying to push its

way through the lace and lifted her eyes to Aaron's.
She gasped at the rapt fascination on his face, loving the power of being a woman, able to make such
a strong, usually somber, man stare in wonder. Gripping him with her legs but trusting him to hold her,
Kasey crossed her arms over her torso and pulled the
cotton shirt up and over her head. She heard Aaron's
gasp of appreciation.

"You are so damn beautiful," he muttered and
Kasey, in that moment, believed him. She watched
as his hand cupped her breast, his thumb pulling the
lace out of the way so that he could stroke her, all his
attention on that one erogenous spot. And suddenly
nothing was more important than having Aaron between her legs, inside her, filling the empty, lonely
spaces inside her.

Aaron lowered his head and sucked her nipple into
his mouth, rolling the bud between his teeth before
drawing it to the roof of his mouth. He used his lips
and tongue and teeth in a way that was, Kasey was
convinced, designed to drive her mad. She arched her
back, her fingers stabbing his hair, holding his mouth
in place. He couldn't stop, but if he had to, then he
needed to take that mouth south, to kiss her in places
that had been neglected for far too long...

"Baby," Aaron murmured, his mouth moving up,
running his tongue along the cords of her neck, the
scruff on his face propelling fire into her veins. He
shouldn't shave, ever... "God, you feel so good."

Kasey dropped her legs to the ground and scooted
her hands up and under his shirt, needing to feel his

warm skin, to explore those hard muscles. She felt free out here, in the darkness next to the pond. In the house she was reminded of Savannah and that it was a place where she worked, but out here under the cover of night, she was just Kasey, and Aaron wasn't her boss but just a man she wanted with a depth that astonished her.

Kasey pushed his shirt up and over his head, her mouth on his chest, skimming over one flat male nipple, through fine chest hair that covered his pecs and channeled into a dark trail that disappeared beneath his cargo shorts. Kasey followed the arrow, her hand gliding over that hard, hard six-pack and over his harder erection. Man, even covered in fabric he felt so big, so virile, every inch of him screaming that he was a man in the best, most primal way.

Aaron's hands went to work on the button of her pants, pulling the zip down before sliding his finger over her and finding—how did he do that?—where she ached. Kasey tilted her hips up and hooked her calf around his for some additional stability while the world, and everything in it, disappeared.

Aaron's fingers dipped beneath the seam of her panties and pulled them to the side, allowing him easier access to her grooves and folds. One finger slid inside her and Kasey released a strangled cry, half swallowed by Aaron when his mouth covered hers. His tongue picked up the same beat of his finger and she knew that she was close to orgasm, about to tip into that firestorm with or without him.

Aaron freed himself and pushed her pants to the

ground. Walking backward, he sat on the edge of the deep-seated bench, pulling Kasey upward so that she straddled him, her core sliding against his freed shaft, warm and perfectly hard. She gasped and slid across him again before encircling him, lifting him to hold him against her. Aaron's hand on her thigh stopped her from rising and she raised her head to look at him, not sure why he wasn't as desperate to reach completion as she was.

Aaron muttered a curse and looked in the direction of the house. "I have condoms at the house."

Kasey wiggled against his fingers, trying to get her tongue to form the words. "I'm safe...on the pill. And I'm clean. You?"

"Same." Aaron clasped her face with one hand and forced her to look at him. "Even so, we should stop—"

"You don't have to."

That was all the encouragement he needed. Aaron gripped her hips and pulled her down so that the hottest part of her pushed against the hardest part of him again. Kasey couldn't stop her whimper as her hips, without her permission, started to slide against him.

"Use me, baby. God, you're so hot," Aaron whispered, lifting his hands to her breasts, his thumbs playing with her nipples. "Yeah, like that...hot, smooth, sexy."

Kasey felt herself soaring again, as if she were an electrical current, flying along heated wires. Placing her arms behind her head, she writhed against him, needing more, just a little nudge to push her into that all-consuming heat.

Aaron provided that nudge when he dropped his hand and sank his finger into her folds, rolling her clitoris under his thumb. Kasey's small scream broke the night and she arched her back, remaining utterly still as wave after wave of pleasure crashed over her. Shuddering, she wrapped her arms around his waist, desperate to hold on to those last remnants of pure, golden pleasure.

Making Kasey come made him feel like he was Atlas and easily able to carry the world.

Aaron sat straighter and wrapped his arms around her, resting his face in her neck. Conscious that he was still full and hard beneath her, he sighed as she pushed her fingers into his hair and murmured in his ear, "You make me feel so good, Air. I want to do the same for you."

God, yes.

But, also, God no.

Aaron silently cursed himself, wishing he could switch off his brain and just be with her. He couldn't use the excuse of her being his employee, she'd told him, through her words and her actions, that she was fully on board with anything, possibly everything, he wanted to do to and with her.

No, Kasey wasn't the problem, he was.

Aaron placed his hands on her hips and lifted her off him, keeping his hands on her until she was steady on her feet. Rising, as well, he tucked himself back into his pants before picking up her pants off the grass and shaking them out. Kasey adjusted her panties, took her pants and stepped into them. She pulled her shirt over her head and looked around for her sandals.

A few minutes passed, Kasey frowned and Aaron knew that she was feeling uncomfortable, possibly pissed off. He couldn't blame her. After Aaron pulled his T-shirt over his head and jammed his feet into his flip-flops, he lifted his head and looked at her.

"I swear, if you mention our working relationship, I might have to hurt you." Kasey said, sounding resigned and, well, sad.

"I'm sorry, Kase. I know I'm blowing hot and cold, but I can't do this."

Kasey looked irritated and gestured to the still-rigid erection tenting his pants. "Excuse me if I don't agree with that stupid statement."

Aaron pushed an agitated hand into his hair. "Of course, I can do it. I just don't feel like I should!"

"As far as I am aware, we are both consenting, unattached adults. There is no reason why we can't have wild monkey sex as often as we like."

Except that it wasn't just monkey sex, that he could handle. It was the emotional connection he was in danger of making during said wild sex that scared him spitless.

He couldn't take that risk. Not again.

But he couldn't tell her that so he used another, equally valid excuse. Aaron pointed to the end of the driveway and to the high ornate gates leading to the road. "Somewhere out there is my brother and he's in a world of hurt. In that house is his daughter, who is confused at best and whose world might be torn apart for the second time in two years. She's getting attached to you, and that's problematic.

"I need to find out what's going on with my brother. I need to make Savannah feel as safe and secure as possible. I do not need to lie awake veering between fantasizing about you naked and crawling all over me and what I'm going to say at my brother's funeral."

Aaron sank to his haunches, his forearm across his bended knee, his head bowed. It was the first time he'd voiced his biggest fear aloud and he prayed that Kasey wouldn't brush his fears aside or urge him to be optimistic. Kasey dropped to the grass, sitting cross-legged in front of him, and placed her hand on his arm. "Is that what you think, Air? Do you think he's dead?"

Aaron lifted his head to look at her. Empathy, not empty sympathy, thank God. "Yeah." His voice sounded like he'd used sandpaper on his vocal cords. "I think he's dead."

Kasey just dropped her forehead to his arm, some-how knowing that small gesture of comfort was all he could deal with.

This amazing woman deserved his honesty, it was all he could give her.

"It would be so easy to lose myself in you, Kase. If we slept together again it would be so easy to pretend that this situation—you in my bed and living in my house—is real and the rest of it isn't." Aaron touched her head, unable to stop himself from playing with her hair. "It's a stressful situation and it's too easy to use you, to use the attraction between us, to hide. And there's the chance we'll start to think that something built on stress and sex and lust is real, when it's not. I can't do that. It's too dangerous. I have a child and a business to protect, a new normal to find.

"What I have to give isn't enough for you, Kasey. You deserve better."

Kasey didn't say anything and Aaron stared down at her head, waiting for her to respond, to chew his head off or to tell him that she understood. Kasey eventually lifted her head and sat back, the balls of her hands pushing into her temples. "One of the things I most admire about you is your honesty. After all the lies of the last few years, and despite the embarrassment factor of throwing myself at you, I am grateful for that."

"So, we're okay?"

Kasey shrugged. "Yeah, we're okay, Aaron."

He wasn't completely convinced but, feeling completely shattered, he'd take her half-hearted assurance. Aaron stood and held out his hand in a silent offer to help her up. Kasey placed her hand in his, allowed him to tug her to her feet and immediately pulled her hand from his. "It's getting late and we ought to head back."

Aaron nodded. "Yeah, I still need to read your wind turbine research and make a decision about investing in that copper mine."

Back to business, Aaron thought glumly, a safe, neutral topic.

They started walking toward the house and Aaron

whistled for the puppies. When the two bandits didn't appear, he whistled again and released a concise, one-word curse. "Dammit! Where the hell are they?"

He looked toward the house, saw two dark forms in the lounge and that they were fighting over a brightly colored shoe box. The box that held Kasey's brand-new trainers. Aaron released a curse and started to run.

Aaron pulled himself through the water, his arms aching and his thighs burning. After less than two hours' sleep, his normal gym session and forty-five-minute swim was punishing.

Reaching the side, Aaron did a quick, professional turn and flipped over onto his back, glaring up at the blue sky as he pulled himself through the water. Swimming was normally the time when he could check out, but all he could think about was the bliss on Kasey's face as she rode him, the moonlight on her creamy skin, the warm, sexy smell of her arousal, that keening sound she made when she came. Not throwing her over his shoulder and running her back to the house and straight into his bed was the hardest decision he'd ever made, but it had been, was still, the right one.

Aaron knew that Kasey wanted him, possibly as much as he wanted her, but they were both adults and, as such, were old enough to realize that you didn't, or shouldn't, always get what you want.

Aaron slapped the wall, turned and belted back down the pool. Kasey intrigued him, made him want to dig beneath her layers to see what was below. And

when he hit that layer, he wanted to dig down another...
He suspected that Kasey was the type of woman you
could spend a lifetime exploring and never be bored.
For a man with a low tolerance for boredom, she was
exactly the type of woman he'd look for...

If he was looking. Which he absolutely wasn't. He
freely admitted that she was a confusing mixture of
smart and sassy, vulnerable and proud, all contained
in a very pretty package.

She also had the ability to melt his defenses, to
decimate his control. And, maybe, that was the real
reason he'd stood on the brakes last night, why he'd
walked away from the offer in her eyes.

She made him lose control and forget, or dismiss,
the hard lessons he'd learned about women and commitment and why he should keep himself emotionally detached.

His attraction to her wasn't only physical, he was
fascinated by her brain, her past, and wanted to learn
about how she came to be the person she was. Curi-
osity and attraction were a volatile combination and,
as he'd learned with Kate, he'd be the one caught up
in the explosion. Aaron had survived one blast, he
wasn't fool enough to look for another.

Besides, a woman and a relationship was so far
down his list of priorities it wasn't even on the page.

Out of the corner of his eye he saw Kasey walk
onto the pool deck, dressed in a pair of denim shorts
and a white, billowing cotton shirt that edged down
one shoulder, showing off a pale pink bra strap. Last

night's creation had been pale green. Aaron wondered how many matching sets she had and in what colors…

Kasey took a sip from the cup in her hand and waited for him to power his way to the end of the pool. When he reached the wall, he dropped his legs and stood.

"Hey."

Aaron pushed his hair off his face and nodded. "Hey." *Scintillating conversation, Phillips.*

"I just came down to tell you that I have to run to town. I need to pick up Savvie's birthday cake and supplies for the party later."

God, he'd forgotten that it was Savannah's sixth birthday party and that his house was about to be invaded by twenty giggling girls for a Princess Pool Party. How the hell had that slipped his mind since it was all Savannah could talk about lately? And, talking about his niece…where was she?

Kasey answered his question. "Hannah's mom offered to take her this morning so that we could run errands. Apparently trying to set up a kid's party with an excitable six-year-old running amok requires the skill of a five-star general or years of practice," she said, sitting on the closest lounger.

Aaron boosted himself out of the pool, his eyes on her face. Twin blue stripes ran under her eyes and her face looked a little pale. So he wasn't the only one who hadn't gotten much sleep last night.

He snagged a towel from behind her, beads of water from his body dropping onto her thighs and feet. Looming over her, and thanks to her blousy top, he had a perfect view down her chest. Yeah, yeah, he shouldn't, but he couldn't resist.

Kasey slapped her hand against her chest and cut off his view. His sighed his disappointment and looked into her irate, whiskey-colored eyes.

"Seriously?" she asked, jumping to her feet.

Aaron shrugged as he wrapped a towel around his waist. "I'm a guy, it's what we do. And you're beautiful."

Kasey threw up her hands and Aaron jumped back as warm coffee hit his stomach and chest. Kasey released a low "Dammit!" and banged her cup onto the closest table, slapping her hands on her hips. Aaron saw determination cross her face and wished he'd kept his mouth shut.

"I'm done, Aaron. This isn't working."

Oh hell, no. If she told him that she was leaving, she would drop him, and Savannah, in a world of hurt. He was normally reticent to the point of rudeness and never ran his mouth, so what in the bloody hell had gotten into him?

"We need to come to an understanding," Kasey stated, her tone suggesting that he not argue with her. "This hot and cold can't go on."

Fair point. Aaron held her eyes and rolled his hand in a gesture for her to continue. "I haven't slept, Aaron, partly because I felt so damn guilty about last night. That I…had, um—you know!"

A small part of him was amused at her blush, at her incoherence when talking about sex. God, her husband had to have been a selfish prick. "Because you came and I didn't?"

Kasey didn't look grateful at his attempt to help her out. "Yes, *that*. You were left high and dry."

Aaron shrugged. He was a big boy, he'd coped. Taking care of himself wasn't much fun but it had helped...sort of.

"And, judging by the fact that you can't resist looking down my shirt and I am standing ten feet away from you because I can't jump you from here, this crazy attraction isn't going away!" Kasey pushed her hands into her hair and scowled. "Why now? We've had eight months together, why didn't it happen sooner?"

That was a no-brainer. "We didn't eat, work and live together, Kase. We hardly saw each other."

Kasey pulled a face. "Oh...right. And now the opposite is true."

Aaron nodded. "Seeing you in those sexy shorts and your flirty sundresses doesn't help," he added.

Kasey pointed a finger at him, waving it in the direction of his chest. "And I see you half-naked every morning. God, you're ripped."

Aaron saw the heat in her eyes and under his towel his junk jumped to life. Yeah, he liked the fact that she thought he was hot, but it didn't help in his quest to keep his hands to himself. Dammit.

"Aargh!" Kasey wailed. "You see, we both do it! You look down my shirt and I get distracted by your abs and those sexy muscles."

Aaron frowned. "What muscles?"

"These sexy hip muscles…" Kasey slapped her hands against her edges of her flat stomach before closing her eyes in frustration. "Seriously, I need a filter on my mouth."

Aaron picked up the T-shirt he'd left on the back of the lounger and pulled it over his head. When the shirt covered his stomach and his, apparently, sexy hip muscles, he quirked an eyebrow at her. "Better?"

Kasey glared at him. "Careful, your ego is showing." She gripped the edge of the wooden table behind her and nodded. "But yes, thank you. Marginally better. So, as I was saying…this can't go on, Aaron. As you know, from last night and my inability to construct a decent sentence this morning, I want you. And I'm pretty sure that you want me, too."

Only with every damn breath he took. "I shouldn't, but I do."

Kasey tipped her head to the side. "And we both agree that this is just about physical attraction, that neither of us needs, or wants, anything more?"

Aaron nodded, not trusting himself to speak. Was she really going there, about to suggest that they have a no-strings affair? Did he want that? Hell, yes. Could he handle it? Could he do a no-strings with Kasey?

That, he didn't know. That was his biggest fear. He didn't want to become emotionally entangled with her and it felt like he could, if he let himself. Sleeping with her would be like opening the door to that possibility. And man, he'd hate it if this fling caused her any pain down the line.

"What if we just explored this, did it a couple of

times, let the fire burn itself out?" Kasey said. "And maybe try to do it in a bed this time?"

Only Kasey could find the humor in this awkward situation. Only Kasey would be brave enough to lay her cards on the table. Aaron appreciated her unflinching honesty, her ability to look at the situation and find a way to deal with it.

Kasey tossed her hair, her eyes still holding that fierce light of determination. "Because it will burn itself out, Aaron. It has to."

Aaron folded his arms and just looked at her. Yeah, the determination blazed hot and true, but beneath that emotion he could see want and need and more than a little fear. She wanted him but she was scared to feel this way. She spoke easily of a sexual relationship, but he had to make it very clear that there would never be anything else, that he had nothing to give her more than some hot nights and explosive pleasure. Or was he trying to convince himself? Hell if he knew. But the words needed to be said; he didn't want any misunderstandings down the line.

Before he could find his words, Kasey plowed on ahead. "If we do this, then it's on the understanding that there will be no hard feelings if one of us calls it quits. No sulking, no temper tantrums, no snide comments. Just a promise to respect the decision and to go back to normal."

Would anything be normal afterward? He wasn't banking on it. He just planted his feet and lifted his eyebrows, knowing she had more to say.

"We still have a child in the house, so, by sunrise, we're in our own beds."

"Obviously," he replied.

"No one knows about this but us."

"That goes without saying."

Kasey shook her head. "I just don't want everybody to know that I'm sleeping with my boss, and you're the one who is connected to the people in this town. Hell, you're a member of the Texas Cattleman's Club."

Despite the wave of anticipation and excitement coursing through him at the thought of, finally, having her again, her comment irked him. "I'm not in the habit of blabbing about the woman I'm sleeping with, Monroe."

"Good to know," Kasey replied, ignoring his irritation. "No spooning when we're clothed. No casual physical affection. No flowers or pet names."

The demands kept sliding off her tongue, as easily as if she were reciting facts she'd garnered for him on a company or a stock. The thought hit him like a bolt out of the blue. Had she researched this? Taken advice from the internet on how to conduct a no-strings affair? Aaron narrowed his eyes. Yeah, he suspected that his very efficient assistant had spent part of the night doing online research. Aaron was partially amused and partially pissed off.

"No expectations, no commitment, no fighting." Kasey kept rolling through her list.

"Are you done yet?" Aaron interrupted her, keeping his voice neutral.

Kasey thought for a moment and nodded. "I think that's it. Is there anything you want to add?"

"Oh, do I actually get a say?" Aaron asked and waited until she nodded. "I'm honored."

Kasey's eyes flashed with indignation. "Don't be snippy."

"Don't be bossy," Aaron retorted. She didn't like taking orders, he suddenly realized. She did it, it was part of her job description, but Kasey preferred to be the one calling the shots, leading instead of following. He'd always been attracted to strong women. He became easily bored with people, men and women alike, who blindly followed where he led. Actually, come to think of it, since Kate, had he deliberately chosen women who were submissive, subconsciously giving himself an excuse to bail? Hmm, interesting.

"Well, what are your conditions? Once we know where we stand, we can talk about when and where," Kasey said, sounding impatient.

Oh, no, that wasn't the way this was going to happen. Their affair was not going to be something scheduled and monitored. If sex didn't happen organically, as a natural consequence to whatever situation they were engaged in, it wasn't happening. Kate had tried to control him using sex, there was no way he was going to let that happen again.

"Two things," Aaron said, walking over to her and only stopping when he was close enough to smell her delicate scent, to feel the tips of her breasts against his chest. He caught her chin in his hand and tipped her face up so that she had to gaze into his eyes. Her mouth looked so damn inviting and her scent enveloped him, his hands wanting to pull her shirt up and over her head, to drop those shorts and plunge inside her. Telling himself not to be a complete moron, he miraculously managed to tamp down his desire.

"This isn't a business deal or a stock trade. We'll sleep together when it feels right, when we are so hot for each other that we can't stand not to," Aaron told her.

Kasey tried to pull her chin out of his hand but he held firm. He looked for any signs of her feeling intimidated but her eyes only flashed annoyance. And underneath the aggravation was hot and potent desire. And maybe, or was he imagining this, the smallest hint of amusement at his grasp for control of this situation. Reassured, he dropped a hard, openmouthed kiss on her lips before speaking again. His second statement was designed purely to annoy her, a small punishment for forcing the issue, for making him face up to the fact that he had no hope of resisting her. "And I'm the boss. In bed and out."

He heard her exasperated gasp as he dropped his hand and stepped away from her, turning to walk into the house. At the doorway, he stopped and turned to look at her, still gripping the table like her life depended on it. She looked frustrated and irritated and turned on and pissed off, a combination that nearly had him heading back to her. He knew she was hot and wet and knowing that he could, within a minute, be sliding inside her warm, secret places filled him with awe.

Kasey held his hot look but Aaron could see the flutter of her pulse in her neck, the heated flush on her cheeks. Aaron wasn't even sure whether she knew that she licked her lips. Was she imagining him picking her up, tossing her over his shoulder and storming up the stairs with her?

It was a hot fantasy, and one he intended to play out in the near future, but unfortunately that would have to wait.

He wanted to smile at her sour-lemon face but he kept his expression inscrutable. Just to keep her off balance, he tossed another conversational grenade at her feet. "I'll come with you and help you with your errands. Shall we leave in thirty minutes?"

"Do I have a choice?" Kasey demanded.

He knew she was really asking about his previous statement, about being the boss in the bedroom. He grinned. "Not even a little one."

Six

The journey back to Aaron's house was quiet and Kasey leaned forward to adjust the stream of cold air pouring out of the air-conditioner vents. She darted a look at Aaron and saw that he was looking at her, that infuriatingly sexy half smile on his face.

He looked confident and relaxed, everything Kasey wasn't feeling since she was having second, and third and fourth, thoughts. Should she tell him that she was unsure? She opened her mouth to speak but then he placed his hand on her bare thigh, his thumb drawing patterns on her bare skin.

Nope, she wanted this, she wanted him. No doubts allowed…

Kasey heard her distinctive ringtone, surprised to see that her phone had synced with the onboard display on Aaron's dashboard. She immediately recognized the number on the screen. Before she could tell Aaron to disconnect the call, he hit the button on his steering wheel and answered, his voice as steady and calm as always. "Phillips here."

After a beat of silence, Dale's voice filled the car. "I'm looking for Kasey. Who the hell are you and why are you answering her phone?"

Irritation flashed across Aaron's face and Kasey dived for her bag, trying to find her phone to cut off the call. "I'm her boss. Who the hell are you and what do you want?"

"I'm her husband. I want to talk to Kasey."

Kasey pulled the bag onto her lap as Aaron whipped the SUV into his driveway, stopped in front of the gates and pressed the remote control on his visor. The gates opened and Aaron steered the car up the long driveway. Anger suffused his face. "I thought you were divorced," he muttered, looking at her.

"I am," Kasey replied. Giving up her search for her phone, she ran a hand over her forehead. "What do you want, Dale?"

"Just a damned conversation. Is that too much to ask?" Dale tacked on a foul curse at end of his statement and Aaron's hands tightened on the steering wheel.

"Watch your mouth, moron," he growled.

"Dale, I'm hot and tired, and I really don't want to spoil my day talking to you," Kasey said.

"Listen, we need to discuss what happened, why our marriage ended. You need to understand that—"

Kasey looked at Aaron and slashed her hand across her neck. Aaron immediately disconnected the call and then pulled his car into his huge garage. He shut off the engine and sent Kasey an inscrutable look before getting out of the car and walking around the hood. However, instead of opening the back door to pick up the bags of supplies, as she'd expected, he yanked open her door, put his hands around her waist and physically lifted her from the vehicle.

Not allowing her feet to hit the floor, he leaned her up against the side of the car and crushed his mouth to hers, silencing the protest she was about to make. His tongue invaded her mouth, and all thoughts of Dale and what he wanted, or could want, and the heat and frustration of the day, melted away. There was only Aaron and he was kissing her, his hand moving up and under her short dress, long fingers digging into the soft skin on the inside of her thigh.

Aaron lifted his head and bent his knees so that he looked directly into Kasey's eyes. "You and me, Kase. I don't want you thinking about anything else except the way I make you feel."

Kasey nodded and Aaron went in for another kiss but her fingers on her lips halted his progress. "That goes for you, too. For a couple of hours, you have to stop worrying about Jason and Savannah." She repeated his words back to him. "There's just you and me."

Aaron pushed a strand of hair off her forehead and tucked it behind her ear. She saw gratitude in his eyes and tenderness. "Deal."

Kasey lifted her mouth to his, tracing her lips across his, the scruff of his beard tickling her in wickedly sensuous ways. "Let's get inside where it's cool," she suggested.

"I know the best place, and it's been a fantasy of mine since you first moved in." Aaron grabbed her hand and tugged her toward the entrance to the house.

Kasey looked back at the car, thinking of the birthday cake and Savannah's party supplies. "The cake will melt," she protested.

Aaron sighed, released her and opened the back door. Handing her a grocery sack, he lifted the Princess cake with one tanned hand and picked up the handles of the other bags. Jerking his head in a follow-me-and-hurry-the-hell-up gesture, he strode into the house. Putting the cake in the cool oven where it was protected from the psycho canine twins, he took the bag from Kasey and dropped them all on the granite surface of the island. Then, holding her hand in his, he led her onto the outdoor patio.

Kanga and Roo barked their hellos and danced around them, but Aaron ignored the puppies, tugging Kasey toward the pool. At the edge of the pool, he kicked off his shoes, swooped Kasey up into his arms and jumped into the refreshing water. As her head broke the surface, before she had time to protest, Aaron pulled her into him, his mouth on hers, startlingly hot compared to the cool water. Realizing that Aaron was standing, Kasey wound her legs around his hips, ignoring the furious barks of the puppies, who had no idea what they were doing.

She did and that was all that mattered. Kasey's dress billowed in the water and she broke their kiss to pull the fabric up and over her head, looking down to see that her white bra and panties were now transparent. Aaron's head was also bent and his hand cupped her left breast, his thumb swiping her nipple through the fabric. Bending his head, he drew it up into his mouth, the fabric an irritating barrier between her and his clever mouth. Kasey used one hand to snap open the front clasp and her breasts were freed to be loved by him.

Wanting him as bare as she was, Kasey pulled Aaron's shirt over his head and allowed it to float away as she ran her hands over his big, broad, muscled shoulders and down his thick biceps. It had been so long since she'd had her hands on him, she wanted to explore every inch of him.

But if he didn't stop tonguing her, driving her wild as he switched from one breast to the other, she didn't think she'd last long enough to touch him at all. Pushing her hand between the band of his cargo shorts and his stomach, Kasey felt Aaron suck in his breath as her hand slid down his pants to encircle his thick shaft. Aaron went statue-still, sucked in a deep breath and laid his forehead on hers.

"God, I want you."

Kasey rubbed her thumb over his tip. "I can tell."

Aaron's hand pushed beneath the fabric of her bikini panties and his long fingers moved between her legs from behind and delved into the hot space between her legs. "You want me, too."

Kasey groaned as he found her bud and gently rubbed it. She arched her back and closed her eyes. "So much," she admitted, her voice low and hoarse. "I can't wait to have you inside me."

"Same here." He pressed a kiss to her forehead. "Do you trust me?"

With this, she did. She trusted him to make her feel wonderful. But she didn't trust him, or anyone, with her heart. "God, yes."

Aaron didn't waste any more time. He released her to undo the button on his pants, then kicked them away. Grabbing Kasey's wrist, he moved her to the side of the pool, to where the water came to his waist. He pushed her panties over her hips and when they were free, he placed both his hands behind her knees, spread her open and pushed into her. Kasey hooked her legs around his back, her heels digging into his butt cheeks.

The shock of pleasure danced through her as he filled her, quickly to be replaced by those insistent waves of pure bliss. Kasey felt herself building up, Aaron's sure, hard strokes taking her to the edge of the abyss. As soon as he felt she was about to tip over, he pulled back, keeping his hips still as he teased her mouth and her breasts. He was taking his time, driving her crazy, building her up and pulling her back. When she thought she had to come or lose her mind, Kasey wound her fingers in his hair, jerking his head back so that he had to look into her eyes.

"Now. Take me now," she ordered.

"Who said you were the boss?"

Kasey tried to come up with a smart-aleck reply but before she could, Aaron was pounding into her, rubbing the base of his shaft along her most sensitive spot and lifting her up, up, up. She was about to scream her frustration when he stilled, thinking he was pulling back, but then he lunged up and into her and Kasey felt herself tumbling, tumbling, exploding, realizing.

Stars exploded behind her eyes, galaxies formed and dissolved as the Big Bang started and ended along every one of her nerve endings. Aaron groaned and from a place far, far away, Kasey felt him tense and then release himself inside her. Holding him tight, she rode another wave of pleasure before dropping her head back and encountering the edge of the pool.

A warm, wet tongue licked her from the edge of her mouth to her temple and Kasey opened her eyes to look up into a pair of quizzical brown eyes. Kanga barked in her face and Kasey felt, and smelled, his warm puppy breath on her face.

Aaron's laugh rumbled over her as he placed his hand under her head and pulled her face into his neck. "I think the puppies had quite a show," he said, amused.

"I hope they aren't scarred for life," Kasey replied as he detached himself from her.

"I'm sure they'll be fine," Aaron said, turning his head to softly kiss her lips. "Kase, that was…"

He didn't seem to be able to find the words but his face told her that he'd loved making love as much as she had.

"I know, it was amazing," Kasey whispered, her breasts rubbing against his chest. She dropped her feet to the floor of the pool and slicked her hands over her head, pushing her hair back. Aaron reached for her hand to pull her back into his embrace, tucking her against his side as he rested his back against the wall off the pool, bending his knees so that the water covered his shoulders. "This water is divine."

Kasey placed her head on his shoulder, laughing when Kanga pushed his snout into Aaron's neck before resting his chin on Aaron's tanned shoulder. She grinned. "Aw, he just wants to cuddle." She sent him a teasing smile. "I like the way you cuddle, Phillips."

Aaron grinned as he lifted his arm to hook his hand around Kanga's head. "Well, I am a really great cuddler."

Kasey dropped her hand to his thigh and rubbed it in a long, smooth stroke, loving the long, hard muscles under his skin. "You really are. So, would you like to…cuddle…me again?"

Roo, the maniac, barked once before launching himself into the pool, quickly followed by Kanga. Aaron shook his head before turning to look at her. "If by cuddle you mean make love to you until you are boneless, then hell to the yes."

Well, all righty, then, Kasey thought, resting her arms along the side of the pool, laughing as she watched Aaron referee the fight between the puppies over his shorts.

He was, after all, the boss.

Not that she'd ever admit that to him.

* * *

Later that afternoon Aaron stood in the doorway to Kasey's bedroom, watching her shove pins into her hair and smiling at the occasional curse that slipped past her lips. A black, silky dressing gown hit her mid-thigh and was belted at the waist, giving him hints of a strapless lacy bra and that spectacular cleavage he'd tasted and teased. Kasey pulled a pin out of her mouth, jammed it into her hair at the back of her head and whipped around, slapping her hands on her hips.

"He gave you twenty minutes' notice?" she demanded, although she already knew the answer to her question. "Who does he think he is?"

"He's Mark Ward," Aaron replied, leaning his shoulder into the door frame. "He's an investor I've been courting for two years, one of the richest men in the country, and I want to put some of his cash to good use." For the second time in five minutes, he looked at his watch. If they didn't leave in the next fifteen minutes, they were going to be late, and he'd heard that tardiness irritated Ward. "I'm lucky that he called while Megan was still here and that she was happy to take Savvie for the evening."

"I really like your sister," Kasey commented.

"She likes you," Aaron said, thinking about how Kasey and Megan had worked so well earlier to make Savannah's party one the little girl would never forget.

"C'mon, Kase, hurry it up," he muttered. Partly because he didn't want to be late but also because looking at her in that curve-hugging dressing gown was a temptation he was finding very hard to resist.

Kasey glared at him. "You told me we were going out twenty minutes ago. In fifteen minutes, I have showered and dried my hair and even managed to do something with it."

Aaron looked at her piles of meticulously arranged curls and wished he could blow off this dinner, pull her onto that bed and scatter those damn pins all over the room. Rich investor, Aaron reminded himself. Important. He'd had her twice before the party and once during the party when they'd left Megan on kid duty for ten minutes and, God, it had been so damn hot. He should be able to keep his hands off her for a few hours but…nope. Not happening.

Get your head in the game, Phillips.

Kasey sat on the stool in front of the dressing table and picked up a square black box, flicking it open with practiced ease. Picking up a tiny brush, she stroked gray powder across her eyelids. "Why am I involved in this madness? You can go on your own and I can watch an adult movie while working my way through a massive bowl of popcorn."

Aaron lifted an interested eyebrow. "An adult movie?" he teased.

Kasey sent him another scowl. "Something that isn't PG-rated. Something with a lot of ass-kicking and a couple of explosions."

She was an action-movie type of girl. Good to know.

"Mark's wife is a foodie and she's been wanting

to eat at the Glass House for a while. He thought that while he was in Royal, we could meet to see if we click enough for us to explore the possibility of doing some deals together."

Kasey continued to work on her eyes and Aaron was happy to watch her. He just wished she'd hurry it up. "And you couldn't handle him by yourself?"

"I could, but he invited me to bring someone, made it very clear that this was a social evening."

Aaron wanted to ask her why women opened their mouths when they applied mascara but didn't want to hold up the process by talking.

"Where are we going again?" Kasey asked, dabbing her cheeks with blusher.

"The Glass House is an upscale farm-to-fine-dining restaurant situated within the Bellamy, which is Royal's newest, and hippest, resort. It's reportedly getting rave reviews."

"Well, if I don't get to see a hot hero kicking butt, at least I'll get a good meal," Kasey grumbled. She stood and Aaron sucked in a heated gasp. Kasey didn't normally use much makeup—she was naturally gorgeous and didn't need to—but her smoky, sexy eyes were a punch to the stomach. She looked sophisticated and timelessly alluring.

Standing in the doorway, shoulder pressed into the door frame, watching her applying her makeup felt normal; worse, it felt right. It was almost as if he was watching a clip advertising what his future could look like, complete with a stunning woman and a precocious little girl. Aaron rubbed his hands over his face, annoyed with himself. One afternoon of stunning sex and he was already a basket case, allowing himself to fantasize over what could never be.

They'd agreed, made a friggin' pact! They'd agreed to not become emotionally attached, this was a no strings affair, something that would end. Not even twelve hours had passed since that discussion and he was already looking for a ball of twine. No. He wasn't going to let that happen, he wasn't going to put himself in the position of needing her and relying on her.

As much as he liked Kasey, and he also respected the hell out of her, he couldn't trust her, or anyone, with his heart or his life.

"Are you okay?"

Aaron's head shot up at Kasey's quietly stated question. "Fine, why?"

"No regrets?" she asked, looking down at her tube of lipstick.

Kasey had the uncanny ability to sense his unease and he didn't like feeling that exposed.

"I'm fine."

Aaron saw her quick frown at that overused word and knew that he had to distract her from asking a follow-up question. They didn't have the time, and he certainly had no inclination, for any non-superficial conversation. "I'm just regretting that there's no time to make use of your bed."

Kasey smiled and his heart flipped over. Aaron sighed, he still really, really wanted to put that bed to good use. To keep from walking across the room and ruining her hard work by kissing her senseless, he glanced at his watch again. They really needed to leave, mostly because he was five seconds away from blowing Ward off altogether.

Kasey walked into the huge closet, pulling the door closed behind her. God, wanting her was killing him, inch by heated inch. Despite their earlier interludes, he wanted to spend the night taking his time, rediscovering every creamy inch of her. It had been ninety minutes but it seemed much longer since he'd touched her. Feeling, attraction, flat-out desire slapped him with the force of a sonic boom. He loved the tender skin behind her ear, hearing her sharp intake of breath when he nibbled her collarbone. Her birthmark low on her back that looked, and tasted, like a strawberry. Her long, finely muscled legs, her sensitive, pretty toes. And all those feminine secret folds that held her passion, her essence, that seemed to crave his touch.

Aaron rested his forehead on the door frame, conscious of the throbbing and rock-hard pipe in his pants. Yay, all he needed was to meet Ward with a hard-on—that would make a good impression.

Forcing his thoughts elsewhere, Aaron recalled the day, and remembering Kasey's devastated face when she'd heard her ex's voice in his car was an effective way to diminish his hard-on. He believed her when she told him that she was over her ex but she was still dealing with their betrayal. Hey, Aaron wasn't about to judge her, a decade had passed and he still hadn't come to terms with his parents' deaths and Kate's duplicity. But Kasey only allowed him glimpses of her pain, only revealed the first layer of her despair but refused to allow him to dig any further.

That he wanted to know more, a lot more, about her irritated him. She fascinated him, always had, right from the beginning, and he'd only managed to keep things professional because he'd valued her sharp mind and business skills. And because they had, despite working closely together, worked out of separate premises. The few times they had met Kasey had walked around with a *Don't go there, it didn't happen* attitude, utterly and completely professional at all times.

But things had changed since she'd moved in here, into his space, and he'd felt the ropes keeping her so tightly controlled loosening. Maybe it was Savvie. Maybe, like him, Kasey had tired of fighting their attraction, but she was thawing...

And, by sleeping together, they'd just stoked the raging fire between them. It had the potential to become an uncontrollable wildfire but he didn't have the faintest idea, or the smallest inclination, to put it out. If he ended up burned to a crisp, it would be his own damn fault.

Kasey stepped out of the closet and Aaron felt his heart quicken. The dress was sleeveless, skimmed her curves and was covered in gold and bronze sequins. And it was short, showing off a lot of her long, slender, spectacular legs. Those legs, the ones he wanted—again!—wrapped around his hips ended in gold-and-black, super-high spiked heels.

Aaron couldn't decide whether to howl his approval or to beg her to change into a nun's habit. He couldn't breathe, but then again, who needed air when he had Kasey to look at?

Kasey picked up a small bag off her bed, tossed in a tube of lipstick and her phone, and tucked it under her arm, a tiny scowl appearing between her eyebrows. "If you don't like what I'm wearing, then tough because I don't have anything else and I would love an excuse to stay here and stretch out in front of the TV."

He wasn't about to say anything. How could he since he'd lost the ability to suck in air? Kasey walked up to him and tapped the watch on his wrist. "Half an hour from soaking wet to ready to rock. You should be impressed, Phillips."

Aaron opened his mouth to tell her he was, that she impressed the hell out of him, but then he saw her bare back and noticed the glittery sequins ended low on her back, just before the flare of her delicious ass.

It was official, the woman was trying to kill him.

Seven

Aaron so owed her, Kasey decided, looking down at her exquisite plate of rare Wagyu beef. Apart from the fact that he didn't make a comment on how she looked—and, dammit, she looked pretty fine—he was also quieter than usual, leaving her to carry the conversation with Mark and his wife. Although naturally quiet, when he needed to, Aaron could work a room with charm and flair and she knew that he was a hell of a conversationalist. The Wards were funny and down-to-earth, despite having squijillions in the bank, and they were a captive audience as she told them what little she knew about Royal and the surrounding countryside.

Kasey took a tiny bite of her beef, sighing her appreciation, as she saw the restaurant manager approaching. While he answered Fiona's questions about the menu and the chef, Kasey took the opportunity to grind her heel into the side of Aaron's foot. As she expected, he pulled away abruptly and narrowed his eyes at her. "What the hell was that for?" he demanded on a low whisper.

"Can you please focus? I'm running out of conversation here!" Kasey muttered, keeping a smile on her face. "What is wrong with you? You need to impress this man and you can't do that if you don't show him that you have a brain underneath that pretty package."

Aaron's mouth quirked up. "You think I'm pretty?"

"Pretty? No. Infuriating, annoying and gorgeous? Yes," Kasey replied. "Just get your head in the game! You're going to lose this opportunity if you don't."

Kasey kept half an eye on the manager and their companions, prepared to give her attention back to them in a heartbeat.

"It's your fault, you know," Aaron said, blotting his mouth with a fine linen napkin to cover his low-pitched words. "That dress could be used as weapon."

Kasey smiled slowly. "You like it?"

"Sure, I like it. But the body inside it is nuclear."

Kasey met his molten green gaze. In his eyes, she could see him naked, rolling her over and sliding into her. "Will you stop doing that?" she demanded, blushing.

"Doing what?" Aaron asked, making a stab at looking innocent. At six-three and built like a running back, it wasn't a look he could pull off.

"Seducing me."

Aaron's big hand covered her thigh, his warm fingers an inch or so from her happy place. "Yeah, that's a problem. Not sure I can do that."

Wanting to throw her arms around his neck and press her mouth to his—something that the smart and sophisticated patrons within the restaurant, and the Wards, wouldn't appreciate—Kasey folded her napkin and laid it on the table. She needed to take a walk, to get some air, to calm the hell down. Bathroom break, she thought. That would give both of them a chance to remember that they were responsible adults and why they were here.

Kasey excused herself, ignoring Aaron's raised eyebrow, and proceeded to saunter across the restaurant, utterly unaware that every male eye in the place was watching her long-legged walk.

And Aaron didn't like that… At all.

"Charming girl," Mark said, swirling the red wine in his glass.

His words only made sense to Aaron when Kasey's heart-shaped butt, long legs and slim frame disappeared from view. Dammit, Kasey was killing his brain cells one chunk at a time. Aaron gave himself a mental punch to the head and met the older man's eyes. He was about to say something innocuous when, surprisingly, another set of syllables left his mouth. "She's driving me nuts."

Fiona laughed and Mark grinned. "We can see that."

Aaron started to apologize and Mark held up his hand, still smiling. "No, please, that wasn't a criticism. Actually it was reassuring to know that you are not a work-obsessed, driven clone. I meet so many of them. Basically they are robots walking around in suits."

He could be like that, Aaron thought, he normally *was* like that. However, in his defense, he didn't think that any man could sit next to Kasey and think of business when she was wearing a dress like that. Feeling his phone vibrate in his jacket pocket, Aaron automatically reached for it, his thoughts immediately going to Jason and then to Savannah.

"My apologies, I do have to check this message." His heart lifted when he realized that it wasn't Megan and that meant everything had to be fine with Savannah. But it sank a second later when he realized the message was from Will. Could it be about Jason? Had they found him? Only one way to find out, Aaron decided, and anxiously opened the message.

Cole and I are at the ranch, brainstorming Jason's disappearance. Care to give your input? Maybe you'll catch something we've missed.

Aaron fought the impulse to stand, call for the bill and head out to the ranch. However, as much as he wanted to do that, he still had a responsibility to his business and he had to drop Kasey off at home. Aaron typed a quick Sorry, could come by later message and tucked his phone away.

He pushed his hand through his hair. "That was rude. I'm sorry, but let me assure you that it is necessary to keep my phone on.

"And I apologize if I've been rude and distracted tonight," he added, keeping his voice even and genuinely apologetic. "It's been an…unusual time and I'm a little unfocused." Not wanting Ward to think that his brain turned to mush at the sight of a pretty girl, he held up his hand. "It's not an excuse but I've had some personal issues that have cropped up."

"Your brother's disappearance for one," Mark said. Aaron was surprised when the gentleman leaned back in his chair, looked him in the eye and murmured, "I wish there was something I could do to help, but I suspect you've done all that you could. I just hope you find him soon."

"Not knowing must be hell," Fiona said, briefly touching his hand with hers.

"It is," Aaron replied. It was easy to talk to these people, he thought, nearly as easy as it was to talk to Kasey. "I'm looking after his daughter, with Kasey's help, and I lie awake at night, wondering what or how I'm going to tell her…"

"Do you think he's in danger?" Mark asked him, straight-out and to the point. Aaron appreciated his not dancing around the issue.

He should just shut up but the steadiness and genuine empathy in their eyes kept him talking. "My heart doesn't want to think that, but my head is telling me otherwise. There's been no activity on his cards, none on his phone. I start thinking the worst and then I feel guilty for losing the faith, telling myself that I can't think like that until I have proof. It's a mess."

Aaron tried to smile and tugged at his collar, wishing he could just stop the words from tumbling from his mouth. It was because these people reminded him of his parents, he realized. They listened to him the same way, both of them tuned in and focused. Damn, that was the first good memory he'd had of his parents in a long, long time.

Aaron sighed. "Honestly, I shouldn't have agreed to dinner tonight. Coupled with Kasey in a sparkly dress…and I'm distracted. I'm better at investing money than my performance tonight shows."

Mark shook his head. "Your reputation and résumé speak for themselves, Phillips. I never doubted your ability to manage my money."

Fiona sent her husband a loving look and leaned forward. "Mark likes men who are real, Aaron. He's researched you, as you have him. I can promise you that if you were effortlessly charming, all over him like a rash, he would've walked away from you in a heartbeat. He prefers genuine to fake and the fact that you are sensitive enough to be worried about your brother and confused by a pretty girl is reassuring, not disappointing. My husband doesn't like robots."

Good to know. Aaron ran his finger around the collar of his open-necked shirt, now feeling more than a little uncomfortable at the turn of the conversation. He was happy that it didn't seem like he'd totally blown this meeting but he wasn't thrilled at being called sensitive.

Looking away from Fiona's warm brown eyes that seemed to see way too much, he suppressed his sigh of relief when Mark changed the subject, taking the spotlight off him. His potential client asked him to identify some of the people in the restaurant and Aaron leaned back in his seat, his eyes skipping over the strangers he didn't know. He pointed out a few of the members of the Texas Cattleman's Club, giving Mark a brief background on the movers and shakers in the room.

Aaron looked into the far corner of the room, idly noticing a tall man rising to his feet. Will's back was to him and he thought that his friend must've had a haircut since he'd last seen him, his hair was army short. The rest of his table rose to his feet and, through the crowd, Will turned his head and Aaron noticed that he was wearing glasses with a heavy black frame. Haircut and glasses, Aaron mused wryly, they were definitely getting old.

"More wine, Aaron?" Mark asked.

He looked back to his host, who was holding a bottle of Château Latour Pauillac, one of his favorite vintages. He started to nod, then covered his glass with his hand. "I'm driving us back home so I shouldn't."

And he needed to have all his wits about him if he was going to look at Cole's case notes, discuss Jason's disappearance—

Aaron frowned and looked across the room again, not seeing the tall man he'd thought was Will. The group had left the restaurant, the man he'd mistaken for Will had probably left with them. Because Will was at the ranch, with Cole, talking about the investigation. Last time he checked, Will couldn't be in two places at once.

Too much sex, stress and too little sleep, Aaron thought. He was seeing things.

"Everything okay, Aaron?" Mark asked, looking concerned.

From somewhere deep inside him Aaron pulled up a smile, but seeing that Mark's expression didn't change, he didn't think he was fooling anyone. He shook his head, glanced across the dining area once more and shook his head again. "I think I might be going mad," he said.

"All the best people do," Fiona reassured him, laughter in her voice. "Here comes your girl."

A couple of hours later Kasey thanked Mark for supper and was surprised when, instead of shaking her hand, Fiona held her arms and dropped a light kiss on her left cheek and then her right. "It was so lovely meeting you, Kasey. I do hope we do this again soon."

"I hope so, too. I had a lovely evening, thank you."

Aaron offered to walk the Wards to the entrance of the restaurant, where the valet had their car waiting, so Kasey excused herself to go to the restroom to freshen up. Like the rest of the venue, the restroom was beautifully decorated and in the corner were two wingback chairs covered in what looked to be silk, a delicate table between the two chairs. Her feet were aching and the chairs looked terrifyingly comfortable, but Kasey knew that if she sat, she might never get back up. She was exhausted, mentally and physically wiped out.

Kasey washed her hands, saw that her makeup was

holding up and reapplied her lipstick, jumping when she saw Michelle's reflection in the mirror next to her own. Instead of turning around, Kasey frowned at her reflection. "Are you stalking me?"

"Oh, get over yourself! I was having a drink at the Silver Saddle—"

"Where?"

Michelle looked impatient. "It's the bar adjacent. I heard that Aaron and you were eating at the restaurant and you always visit the restroom before leaving a restaurant, so I took a chance. See how well I know you?" Michelle replied, moving to stand next to Kasey and placing her butt against the counter holding the basins.

Kasey sighed. "Why are you still in town, Michelle?"

"I told you that I was thinking about relocating to Royal for the short term."

"So that you can win me back?" Kasey dropped her lipstick back into her bag and tucked it under her arm.

"Partly." Michelle shrugged. "I like the town and I'm interviewing at Pure, they have an opening for a specialist masseur. I'm waiting to hear whether I got the position."

"Well, if they were interviewing for someone who slept with her best friend's husband, you'd already have the job." The words left Kasey's mouth and she immediately regretted them because tears filled Michelle's eyes and hung, like perfect little jewels, on the bottom row of her eyelashes. When Kasey cried, her eyes swelled and she looked like a piglet, but Michelle looked as perfect as ever.

"When are you going to forgive me, Kase? It was one time. We were drunk. I don't remember any of it. It just happened." Michelle placed her hands on the counter and stared down at the floor. "You've been my best friend since I was ten. I love you and I miss you, but you're so damn stubborn!"

Was she making too big a deal of this? she asked herself yet again. Was she throwing away her best friend because she was making this out to be more than it was? Was she being naïve?

"I was wasted. I remember climbing next to him on the sofa, thinking that I just wanted to be held. I don't remember much else."

Kasey shifted from foot to foot, wanting to walk out but unable to. She rubbed the back of her head. "I don't think you realize how much you hurt me, Mish. What you did was inexcusable."

"I didn't mean to and I was parrot-face drunk. Surely that counts for something? Don't you miss me at all? Is one night worth throwing away everything we meant to each other? We spent every summer together, we chose the same college so we could be together. We shared an apartment. We did *everything* together."

Dale used to complain about the excessive amount of time she and Michelle had spent together, along with frequent barbed comments about the fact that Kasey carried Michelle financially. Michelle was always short of cash and Kasey had bailed her out more times than she could count.

But having Michelle in her life, someone who knew her inside and out, the only link to her past and her grandparents, had been worth the money she'd thrown in her direction. She was funny, loving and kind, and such fun to live with.

Kasey hung her head. "I can't just wipe it away."

"Don't you miss me, miss us?" Michelle whispered.

Kasey couldn't answer her, knowing that if she did, she might just forgive her. She wasn't ready to do that, not just yet. Or maybe she was and that was what scared her more.

Michelle sent her a teary smile, squeezed her hand before walking toward the exit.

Kasey slumped against the counter and winced when she heard a toilet flush and then a door to a stall opening. Blushing, she looked to her right and saw the beautiful and sympathetic face of a woman with her long hair tucked under a white ball cap. Her chocolate-brown eyes radiated sympathy.

Kasey waited for the gorgeous stranger to make a comment but when she stayed silent, she shrugged. "Sorry about that. As you heard, I have the worst taste in men."

The woman nodded as she approached the basin to wash her hands. "And friends."

Kasey couldn't argue with that.

"I'm Danica Moore, by the way, Dani to my friends. I'm the executive chef here at the Glass House."

"I'm Kasey," Kasey told her. "That Wagyu beef was extraordinary."

Pleasure flashed in Dani's eyes. "Thank you, I appreciate that." Dani hesitated before asking her next question. "So, let me get this story straight—your friend slept with your man?"

"Yep, my best friend had a drunken encounter with my husband. They both said that they were too wasted to know what they were doing."

"Ouch." Dani rinsed her hands, her face thoughtful. "But she was sober enough to remember that she was lonely, that she wanted to be held? Forgive me, but that explanation sounds fishy."

Huh, Kasey thought, she hadn't thought of that.

"Her actions hurt you more than your husband's infidelity did," Dani said, drying her hands.

Kasey blinked back her tears. "I want to forgive her and I want her back in my life, but I can't pull the trigger and tell her that."

Dani shook her head. "You don't really want to forgive her. What you really want is for life to roll back to what it was like before."

Kasey thought of being married to Dale and shuddered. No, she far preferred to be around Aaron, big, and self-contained. And so damn honest. She always, always knew where she stood with Aaron. But yes, Dani was right in that she wanted to obliterate any memory of what Michelle had done or for it to have not happened at all.

Dani touched her shoulder. "Listen, one thing I

know is that you can't look back, you can't live in the past. You have to deal with reality, today. Now."

"Reality blows," Kasey whispered, knuckling away a tear. She glanced at herself in the mirror and just from a few tears her eyes were horror-film red. *Perfect.*

Dani smiled. "Yeah, sometimes it does. But you look like a strong woman who can handle whatever is sent your way."

"I need to get back to work," Dani added as they walked out of the restroom. She glanced at Kasey and grinned. "You really don't cry well, honey. You look all blotchy and orange-eyed."

"Thanks," Kasey retorted.

Dani smiled and held up her hands. "Sorry, I call it as I see it. On that note, I know that you don't want to hear this…but your friend? She's playing you. Be careful, Kasey."

Yeah, that was exactly what she didn't want to hear.

Aaron woke up with the early-morning sun in his eyes and buried his face in the crook of Kasey's neck, holding her naked body close to his. She was his perfectly matched puzzle piece, her head under his chin, her bottom curled into his groin, his legs tucked beneath hers. After more than a decade of waking up alone, holding her, breathing her in, felt good, Aaron thought. It felt *right*.

The last time he'd felt this content, even happy, with a woman was in those early days with Kate, before she'd screwed him over. Kasey was Kate's intellectual equal but his ex didn't have a fraction of Kasey's natural warmth. Kate had only one priority, her own well-being, while Kasey put everyone else's needs before her own. Kasey wanted to believe the best of people. Why else would she be trying to find an excuse to reboot her friendship with her best friend?

Aaron was a black-and-white type of guy while Kasey saw the world in shades of gray, he thought, cupping her soft, warm breast in his hand. Despite being hurt and betrayed, she was far more tolerant than he was and that made her vulnerable. Something about her friend moving to the same town Kasey had relocated to, the way she kept "bumping" into Kasey, made him leery and suspicious. It was almost stalker-ish...

Aaron frowned, acknowledging there was a strong possibility that her friend might hurt her again. And if that happened, he would kick some ass. Nobody, including him, would hurt Kasey if he could prevent it. There had been too much failure in his life: he'd hurt his parents, he'd allowed Kate to play him, he'd failed to protect Megan from Will's impostor...

Well, Kasey *would* be protected, no matter what it took. Maybe he could get Cole, or one of his associates, to look into Michelle and her life, to see if there was some ulterior motive behind her behavior...

But was that going a step too far? They were sleeping together, just having sex, she didn't need or want him interfering in her life and snooping into her friend's motives was way over the line they'd drawn in the sand.

Aaron sighed, thinking that, as per usual, nothing was ever simple. He and Kasey were supposed to sleep together and extinguish his fire for her, but his desire for her was nowhere near close to burning out. Yeah, sex was a brilliant distraction from his fears about Jason's safety and raising Savannah on a full-time basis, but every time he slept with Kasey he felt closer to her, emotionally as well as physically. With every kiss, he wanted more, wanted to sink into her strength, open up to her about his past and his fears…

He didn't know if he had it in him, but for the first time in…well, forever, he felt the urge to trust *somebody.*

Kasey wiggled in his arms and he heard her yawn.

"I can hear you thinking," she complained.

Aaron placed his lips in her hair. "Sorry, baby."

Kasey stroked his forearm. "Don't apologize, I know how much you have on your mind."

"Actually, I was thinking about you and your friend," Aaron admitted.

Kasey rolled over onto her back, her whiskey-colored eyes puzzled. "Why?"

Aaron pushed a strand of hair out of her eyes. "I don't trust her."

Kasey's smile didn't reach her eyes. "You don't trust anyone."

Aaron opened his mouth to tell her his earlier thought, that he was on the point of trusting her, but self-preservation had him pulling the words back. "Just like you."

"I trust you more than I do anyone else," Kasey admitted, turning on her side to face him. Her hand drifted over his hip and he felt the blood drain from his head.

"Ditto, honey." Aaron dropped his mouth to hers, pushing the words out against her lips, knowing that they had to be said. "But I'm giving you as much as I can."

Or, he silently amended, as much as he'd allow himself to. Because if he handed over his trust, his heart…if he laid it all at her feet and she stomped on it, he didn't think he would recover. Kasey wasn't the kind of woman a man recovered from.

She curled her arm around his neck, sadness in her eyes. "I know you are and I'm not ready for more, personally. But professionally…?"

Aaron frowned at her, puzzled. "Yeah?"

"This is probably the wrong time to bring this up, seeing that I am naked and we're not in the office, but—" Kasey wrinkled her nose and shook her head. "Forget it, it'll keep."

Aaron shook his head, intrigued. "No, go for it. Say what you think."

Kasey sat up and pulled the sheet over her chest, hiding her pretty breasts from his view. Holding the sheet with one hand, she tucked her hair behind one ear, then the other. Taking her time, she wiggled her butt before blurting out the words. "It hurts that you don't trust me with the names of your richest clients.

Every time I enter their stupid code words into the system, when I'm capturing data, it's like standing on a rusty nail. I would never release that information, Aaron. Those names are safe in my mouth, in my hands."

Aaron pushed himself up, surprised by her vehemence. "I didn't realize it bothered you so much."

Kasey lifted her slim shoulders. "It shouldn't but it does. I'm big on honesty. I pride myself on my integrity and I've worked for you for eight months. You not trusting me fully, on a professional basis, stings."

Aaron rubbed his stubble-roughened jaw, turning her words over in his mind. If he was in the same position, would he feel the same? Probably, he admitted. "It's not you, Kase, it's me."

Her amber eyes darkened with annoyance at what she thought was a cop-out. He held up his hand, silently asking for her to wait, to listen. He'd never told anyone about Kate, preferring to keep his broken heart and dented pride to himself. He just needed a minute to work out what, and how, to explain.

"I was trading in the last year of college and my—" how to describe Kate? "—*partner* and I were very successful, very quickly. About six months before I was due to graduate, I dropped out to focus on the business. My folks died unexpectedly and a few months after that, my partner absconded from the business, taking our clients and leaving me with nothing." He released a breath. "Long story short? I've worked with numerous people over the years, done many deals, had a few employees. I've never told anybody who my top ten are."

Kasey smoothed the sheet over her thighs, her head bent. After a long time, she lifted her head and tried to smile. "I understand. I do, I know what it feels like to be betrayed. But…"

"I'm sorry." Aaron placed his hand on her knee. He dropped his head to place an openmouthed kiss on the bare skin of her shoulder. "I want to, Kase, but habits die hard. I don't know if I'll ever get there."

Kasey nodded and when she averted her gaze, regret twisted through him. Desperately wanting to wipe the pain from her eyes, he pushed her onto her back, his mouth touching her lips, her chin, her jawbone. He'd had her a few times last night and he wanted her again. He wanted to make love in the early-morning sunlight, to watch her fall apart in his arms. Because when she left, and she would leave, because nothing wonderful in his life ever lasted, he'd have this memory of her in his bed, sunbeams on her skin.

Kasey's fingers were tap dancing down his spine when he heard his phone ring. He turned his head to look at the offending object and decided, just this once, to let it go to voice mail. He pulled a pink nipple into his mouth, heard Kasey's low murmur of approval and cursed when his phone rang again.

Kasey stretched out her hand, snagged the phone from the bedside table and handed it to him. Aaron looked at screen, saw Cole's name and grumbled in exasperation as he rolled off Kasey. He snatched the device from her hand and barked out a quick hello.

It took Aaron a few minutes to make sense of what Cole was saying. He turned to look at Kasey, who'd wrapped her arms around her bent knees, her expression quizzical. Thinking that he might need her help to make sense of this latest craziness, Aaron told Cole to hold on, switched the phone to speaker mode and asked the PI to repeat himself.

"I was just informed by one of my contacts in law enforcement that there is a link between Rich and a small aircraft crash in the Sierra Nevada mountains a few weeks back. A body was recovered from the wreckage but because the local sheriff deemed it to be an accident, the victim was identified and quickly cremated."

Aaron's eyes met Kasey's, as puzzled as she looked. "What's the connection to Rich?"

"The aircraft's registration number. It matches one in Will's fleet," Cole replied.

Aaron saw Kasey's eyes widen and felt the earth shift beneath his feet. He held out his hand to Kasey and when her fingers gripped his, the room stopped spinning. "Who was the victim?"

"Said to be a Bob Smith," Cole replied. "Apparently he has no next of kin, no friends and was all but broke."

That didn't sound right. "Yet he was flying an expensive light aircraft?" Aaron asked.

"Sounds awful convenient, doesn't it?"

Damn right it did.

"The sheriff did the bare minimum to investigate the crash, the body was cremated without doing an autopsy and the sheriff is being supremely uncooperative," Cole continued.

"His remains?" Aaron asked.

"The sheriff said he and his friends conducted a small ceremony and dispersed of the ashes. I call BS," Cole said. Aaron felt his stomach knot. God, he knew what Cole was implying…

"I'm going to make my way out there, but it's going to take me some time since I'm out of state," Cole stated. "Thanks to jurisdictional crap and territory disputes, it's going to take some time for the red tape BS to be waded through. But if you went up there and nosed around, because you are a civilian, you might get more out of the sheriff."

Finally, he could do something to help. He looked at Kasey. "Get hold of my pilot, tell him to file a flight plan for—"

Cole told him the name of the town and Kasey scrambled out of bed, all long legs and creamy skin. Aaron shook his head—*concentrate, Phillips!*—and turned his attention back to the logistics of their trip. "—Durango City and that I want to leave as soon as we get to the airport, which should be within the next half hour or so. We should reach Durango City sometime after lunch."

"Good enough," Cole said. "Let me know what you find. And, Aaron?"

"Yeah?" he snapped, impatient.

"Watch your back."

Aaron disconnected the call, walked over to his closet, pulled down an overnight bag and a change of clothing. When he turned back to look into the room, he saw Kasey wrapping a towel around her torso. "I need a five-minute shower and another ten to pack, I'll meet you downstairs," she told him, looking determined.

Aaron shook his head. "You're not coming with me."

Kasey didn't react to his no-nonsense tone. "Of course I am. Savannah is at Megan's and your sister will keep her until we get back. I am not letting you fly out on your own, not knowing what you might find."

Stubbornness settled over his face. "You don't know what you are talking about."

"Don't insult my intelligence, Aaron. I know what you are thinking... Air, could the remains from this victim be the same remains in the urn supposedly sent by Jason to Megan with the note saying they are Rich's remains?"

Yeah, Kasey wasn't a fool and she'd made the same connections he and Cole had.

"You thought you saw Will at the Glass House last night but if it wasn't Will, then who looks enough like Will to momentarily fool you? Rich. And if Rich is in Royal, then who died in that airplane crash?"

Aaron couldn't say it, didn't want to think it. "It can't be Jason, Kase. I don't think I can handle it."

Kasey walked over to him and wound her arms around his waist, placing her lips against his heart. "I hope it's not, Air. I pray it's not. But just in case there's a small chance it is, you can't be alone. I won't let you do this alone. I'm going, Aaron, and you're going to let me."

Aaron took a minute to hold her, to suck in the support she offered, thinking that this one time, this one time, he'd allow someone in. And he'd take her prayers and add a few of his own.

Not that he believed, not for a minute, that his prayers would change the outcome.

Eight

Kasey followed Aaron into the small building housing the sheriff's office, trying to keep up with his long-legged stride. It had been a long day already and she was bubbling over with frustration, but her boss, and lover, was a tightly coiled string about to snap.

They'd planned to be in Durango City by midafternoon but thanks to a violent thunderstorm lashing the Sierra Nevada mountains, they'd needed to divert to an off-the-beaten-track landing strip that was just long enough to land Aaron's Gulfstream. Finding a vehicle to rent had been their next challenge. When they finally did, they'd made the journey to Durango City in lashing rain, finally arriving, tense and snappy, in the small town situated in the foothills of the mountain range. Kasey knew that Aaron wanted to visit the crash site but it had also been many weeks since the plane had gone down and Kasey wasn't sure what Aaron was hoping or expecting to find.

Kasey, who was a little more detached from the situation, thought that talking to the sheriff and the game warden who'd happened upon the crash would be more constructive. Maybe they'd stumble onto something, but Kasey wasn't holding her breath. This whole trip was a massive fishing expedition and she doubted they'd hook much, or anything, at all.

Kasey looked at Aaron's tight face and sighed at his bleak expression. *God*, she prayed, *please let there be something, anything.*

Standing at the counter waiting for the young deputy who was also acting as a dispatcher to finish her call, Kasey leaned into Aaron's side. He was as stiff as a plank. She linked her fingers in his and squeezed. "Why don't you let me do the talking? Honey will work better than vinegar or, in your case, homicidal frustration."

He managed a tiny smile and nodded his agreement. Aaron allowing her to take the lead, to do something for him, was a small victory, Kasey realized. He didn't release control easily and when she was alone, later, she'd savor the fact that he trusted her enough to do this for him.

Kasey placed both her hands on the counter and sent the young woman a smile. "Hi, we were wondering if we could speak to the sheriff. Is he in?"

The deputy tossed a look at the closed door across the room and frustration flashed in her bright blue eyes. "It's quitting time and the sheriff doesn't like problems at the end of the day."

Kasey suspected she was trying to contain a massive eye-roll. Her disdain for the sheriff's adherence to office hours was easy to discern.

Feeling Aaron's bubbling anger, she squeezed his hand in warning. "It's about that plane crash up in the mountains a few weeks' back. We won't take much of his time."

"Victim's been identified, case is closed."

The female deputy left the room as Kasey turned around to see a slim man, well-groomed, standing across the room, in front of a door with large writing emblazoned across the glass. Sheriff Billy Orson, she presumed, wearing very nice threads for a small-town cop. Cold-eyed and tense, Kasey thought. And, judging by the long up-and-down he gave them, not at all happy to see them. Kasey pasted on a smile and walked across the room, Aaron by her side. She held out her hand for him to shake but Sheriff Orson kept his hands in his pockets, rudely ignoring her gesture.

Well, then. "My name is Kasey Monroe and we'd like to ask you some questions about the plane crash."

"Nothing to say. It crashed into the side of the mountain. The victim's wallet was in his pocket. Body and photo ID looked alike. Did a search, no next of kin, no fixed abode, no money."

"You didn't find it strange that someone with minimal resources was flying an expensive aircraft?" Kasey asked. "And that the aircraft wasn't registered to him?"

The sheriff looked bored. "People hire planes all the time."

"Can we see your reports? The photo ID, pictures of the man who died in the crash?" Kasey persisted, annoyance at his lack of cooperation turning her voice as sharp as a knife blade.

"No."

"What else can you tell us?"

"Nothing."

Before she could blink, Aaron stepped up to the sheriff and slammed his hand on his chest, pinning him to the door of his office. "Start talking."

Something cold and malicious appeared in the sheriff's eyes. "Take your hands off me or I'm going to arrest your ass!"

"You and whose army?" Aaron growled, not dropping his hand. "You know more than you're saying and I want to know what you're hiding."

"Get your hands off me." The sheriff dropped his hand, pulled out his weapon and placed the barrel against Aaron's chest.

Kasey sucked in a horrified breath but Aaron, nerves of cold steel, just held his eyes.

"Aaron, back off before you get hurt," Kasey snapped.

Aaron kept the sheriff pinned to the door with just the force of his hand on his chest and ignored the gun. "If he shoots me, he has to shoot you, and two dead bodies would be tricky to explain. Drop the gun, moron."

The sheriff dropped the gun to his side but Aaron's

hard eyes didn't waver from his face. "Tell me about the crash."

Kasey saw fear flash in Sheriff Orson's eyes. She thought he was about to speak when he closed his eyes and the color disappeared from his face.

"Nothing to tell." Kasey had to strain to hear his words. "Nothing I *can* tell."

The sheriff was scared of Aaron but there was someone else who scared him more. Kasey looked at Aaron and placed a hand on his arm, silently encouraging him to release his hold on the lawman. They'd get nothing more from him. When Aaron finally dropped his hand and stepped back, she knew that he'd come to the same conclusion.

"You're as shady as hell and you'd better find yourself a damn good lawyer because, if I find out that you are in any way complicit in what happened to my brother, I will chase you into the depths of hell."

This cold, hard man didn't sound like Aaron but it was him; ruthless, determined, dogged. A little scary but ridiculously sexy. Was it weird that his badass attitude made her insanely hot? Yeah, Kasey thought, it was weird.

"We're staying at the local inn tonight, room 14, and we leave at the break of dawn. If there's anything you want to tell me, it had better be before then." Aaron bent his knees and glared into the sheriff's worried eyes. "Trust me, you don't want to mess with me."

Sheriff Orson opened his mouth to speak, abruptly

shook his head and forced his lips to sneer. "Get the hell out of my town."

Aaron didn't react, his hard expression didn't change. "Break of dawn. Don't make me come looking for you."

Kasey, hearing the knock on the door to the honeymoon suite at the Durango City Inn, lifted her head off Aaron's shoulder and frowned at him. He looked at his watch and Kasey turned his hand to squint at the dial. "It's after midnight."

Aaron pulled away from her, stood and quickly pulled on his jeans. He waited at the door until Kasey was dressed in a sweatshirt and yoga pants before pulling it open. She looked past him to see the young deputy from the police station standing in the hallway.

"Can I come in?" she whispered.

Aaron stepped back and the girl slipped into the room, her arms folded against her chest. "I don't have much time. I'm Jen, by the way."

Aaron shut the door behind her and leaned against the wall. "Why are you here, Jen?"

Jen rocked on her heels and Kasey thought she looked like someone had shot her dog. "My dad was the sheriff of Durango City for a long time. When he died, Sheriff Orson was elected."

Kasey exchanged a look with Aaron, neither of them understanding the relevance of her statement.

"My dad was a good cop who believed in justice. Orson is as dirty as an old barn," Jen stated, her eyes flashing with anger. "I grew up with my dad and he spoke to me about his cases, and everything Orson did on this investigation was wrong."

Aaron straightened, his interest piqued. "What do you mean?"

"From the beginning, this case was…fishy. If there's an accident on the mountain, the search-and-rescue team gets called out to recover the body, but Orson and a friend brought the victim back down, on their own. As per policy, I met Orson at the funeral home to collect evidence, but there wasn't any. No photos of the scene, no personal effects, nothing. I heard Orson tell the funeral director that there was no family, no one to contact, and that he should be cremated as soon as possible, and that he would, personally, pick up the cost."

Aaron rubbed his hand over his lower face. "Holy crap."

Jen pulled a face. "It gets worse and that's why I'm here."

Kasey knew that whatever she was about to say was going to rock Aaron's world and there was nothing she could do or say to protect him.

"Later that night I went back to the funeral home and snuck into the room holding the two-man body fridge. My gut was screaming at me to do something. Everything about this situation was wrong and I needed to do right by this victim. I didn't believe, for one second, anything that Orson said."

"What did you do?" Aaron asked, sounding choked.

"I swabbed the vic's mouth for DNA and pulled some strands of hair from him. I sent those samples off to the state forensics lab, faking Orson's signature. I hid the results when I got the DNA report back." She tossed the envelope onto the closest chair. "There's the report, you can compare his DNA against whoever you are looking for." Jen rocked on her heels, looking miserable. "I'm sorry to tell you this, but the man who died in that crash looked a lot like you."

Kasey saw Aaron's knees buckle and his hand reach out to grip the door frame to steady himself. She wanted to go to him but his quick glance warned her to keep her distance.

"There's more—" Jen said.

God, Kasey thought, how much more would Aaron be able to take? "He wore a ring on his finger. It was pretty distinctive," Jen said, looking at the bed where they'd held each other a little while before, back when life still made sense.

"Black tungsten edged with rose gold. Two intertwined hearts engraved on the inside band. He wore it on the ring finger of his right hand, not left," Aaron said, his voice breaking.

Kasey then noticed that Jen held an evidence bag in her hand, filled with two medicine vials and, in the corner, a black-and-gold ring. She lifted it up. "Additional samples of his DNA, in case you want to run more tests. Do you want to keep this? I don't know what to do with it and if I'm found with it I'll lose my job."

Aaron just stared at the bag, so Kasey, her heart breaking for him, took the bag Jen held out. "Thank you," she murmured.

Jen nodded. "I'm so sorry," she said before turning to walk toward the door. "If, at some point in the future, you need me to speak to your local cops, or any other law enforcement, I'm prepared to do that, even if it means losing my job."

Kasey placed the evidence bag on the table, conscious that Aaron's eyes hadn't left the clear plastic packet. "We so appreciate this, Jen."

"There's one more thing I thought was strange. You're from Royal, Texas, right?"

Aaron nodded.

"Well, that's where Orson sent the urn containing the ashes."

Kasey shut the door behind Jen and turned back to look at Aaron, desperately wishing she could find the right words to comfort him, if comfort was at all possible. As she looked for something to say, Aaron sat on the edge of the bed and started to pull on his shoes.

"Where are you going?" she asked him.

"Out."

Kasey looked toward the window and, although it was pitch-dark outside, she could hear the heavy rain slamming against the windowpane. "Okay, give me five minutes to get dressed and I'll come with you."

"I don't need you," Aaron said and, without looking at her once, walked out of the room.

Kasey rested her forearms on her knees and closed her eyes. It was a special type of hell when you wanted to be there for someone you loved but they wouldn't let you in. Kasey tunneled her fingers through her hair and groaned as the full impact of that thought hit her.

She loved Aaron. She did. She loved him unconditionally, probably had from the moment they first met but her brain had taken a while to take on board what her heart, and body, already knew.

She simply loved Aaron with a depth of feeling that astounded her: no strings, no provisos, no conditions. It was something that just was…

Loving Aaron, a man who didn't need or love her back, was now her new reality.

Kasey, despite her efforts to stay awake, drifted off to sleep around 4:00 a.m. and when she woke at seven, Aaron was standing in front of the window, his shoulders up around his ears. Walking over to him, she placed her hand in the middle of his back and rested her forehead on his spine.

"How are you doing, Air?"

It was such a stupid question—he was obviously gutted at the news of his brother's death—but she had to say something. Kasey felt his chest rise and fall with his intake of breath. "I'm…as good as it gets."

Kasey moved to stand in front of him, so that she could see his face. His beard was long past his normal sexy stubble and she could barely see his lips, his mouth was so tightly drawn. And his eyes, his beautiful green eyes, were flat and dull. Kasey placed her hand on his big biceps. She followed his gaze and looked out the window. The clouds had moved on and the mountain range loomed in the distance.

"I faxed the DNA report to Cole. He's going to get the DNA compared to Jason's, and the ashes in the urn Meg received, but there's no question in my mind that it's him. Hearing that he's dead isn't a surprise. Since the moment I heard that he hadn't contacted Savvie, I think I knew in my gut that he wasn't coming home."

"I'm so sorry."

"I have to tell my niece and my sister…" Aaron said, his voice as bleak as those mountains in the winter.

"That's going to be tough," Kasey murmured. She knew it was a long shot but she had to try to keep his hopes up. "The DNA testing might still prove that it's not him, Aaron."

"He never took that ring off, Kasey." Aaron rubbed his face with his hands. "After my folks died, I thought I'd never have to be the bearer of bad news again. I thought that once was enough."

"What do you mean?"

Aaron looked utterly miserable. "I told Jason and Megs that they were dead, that they both were killed in a car accident." The lack of emotion in his voice scared Kasey. He wasn't an unemotional man, he loved deeply, but she sensed that he had to shove down his emotions to function.

"They were on their way to see me and were killed about twenty miles from Stanford. That's the basics, but I never told Jay and Megan that the reason they were in Stanford was to see me."

Kasey sat on the seat of the bay window and looked

up at him, puzzled. Aaron kept his eyes fixed on the mountains and Kasey knew that not looking at her was his way of coping. "I was interning at a small investment firm and I was sleeping with my older boss. I was also in love with her. We were about to open up our own investment firm, she had a couple of clients and I had wealthy contacts back in Royal. I told my folks and they lost it. They jumped into the car to talk some sense into me and they called me to tell me they were nearly in Stanford. The argument started up again on the telephone—I said something about them staying the hell out of my life and then I heard the crash, heard my mom scream."

Kasey shuddered, desperately fighting her tears. But if Aaron could stand there dry-eyed, then she wasn't allowed the luxury of falling apart.

"I not only caused their death—" God, Aaron, no! "—but I also failed them by not taking care of my siblings."

Kasey frowned, trying to work out the meaning of his words. "I don't understand, Aaron."

"I encouraged Megan to marry 'Will.' I walked her down the damn aisle! I didn't spend enough time with Jason, I didn't keep close enough tabs on him."

Kasey understood his irrationality: when things went wrong, blame had to be assigned and Aaron, with his overly heightened sense of responsibility, was blaming himself. "You're not being fair on yourself, Aaron. Megan is an adult as was Jason. They made their own decisions."

Aaron shook his head, his expression pure stubborn pride. "I'm the oldest, I could've done something to prevent all this."

Kasey stood and wrapped her arms around him. "It's not your fault, Aaron. *None* of this is your fault. Not your parents' death, not Megan's marriage, not Jason's death. This isn't your burden to shoulder." Yet, even as she uttered the words, Kasey knew that nothing she could say would penetrate his grief. He needed to mourn, to let go, to feel. Blaming himself was, she thought, maybe easier than dealing with the solid reality that his brother was dead, probably by another man's hand.

He needed to break, Kasey realized, and he needed to expel some of this acidic, corrosive guilt and tension. There was comfort in sex—in being wrapped in warm arms, folded into a heart that loved you. Sexual intimacy might help ease his grief. Like she'd needed sex eight months ago when she'd felt unloved and undesirable, Aaron needed sex right now to disconnect, to release some tension and to be with someone who loved him. He'd deny that need with his very last breath, but Kasey knew that he needed that connection to someone; he'd been alone, truly alone, for far too long. It wasn't a long-term solution, of course, but sex would be a balm on his open, weeping wound, temporary stitches to his broken heart.

Without giving herself time to talk herself out of what she was about to do, she placed her hand on his crotch and felt shock ripple through Aaron. He didn't move but under her fingers, through the denim fabric of his jeans, she felt him harden and knew that he was about to pull away.

Kasey kept her hand on him and stood on her toes to look into his eyes. "You need this, Air. Let me give this to you. Let me take away a little of the pain. It'll come back with a vengeance, but for now... Let me take care of you." She wanted to tell him that she'd always be there for him, as little and as much as he needed, but now wasn't the time or place.

"God, Kase, I—"

Kasey rubbed her thumb up his long length. "You need this, let me give you this."

She pushed her hands under his T-shirt and lifted the material up his chest and over his head. Aaron just watched her, those emotionless green eyes warming slightly as desire temporarily swamped grief. Kasey kissed his sternum, his collarbone, the flat circles of his nipples, her hands tracing the hard ridges of his muscles.

"I love the way you touch me," Aaron muttered.

"I love to touch you," Kasey assured him, knowing her statement to be pure truth. She could do this for the rest of her life, touch this one man, forever. She loved him: it was inconvenient and possibly disastrous, but she'd do anything for him.

Kasey opened his belt, flicked open the top button of his jeans and, one by one, separated the rest of his buttons of his fly. Sliding his jeans down, she quickly discovered he wore no underwear and was glad there were no more barriers to her touch.

She wrapped her hand around his shaft and looked

up at him, his eyes closed and the muscles in his neck and shoulders loosening. She cupped his balls and stroked him from shaft to tip, hoping her touch was all-consuming, allowing him a measure of distance from his grief. Ironic that keeping his distance was what she least wanted from him—she wanted his hopes and dreams and thoughts and worries—but right now, detaching from all those emotions was what she could give him.

Kasey felt his hands on her breasts, thumbs running over her nipples. This was about him but she felt the tug of desire, the need for more. Tilting her head up, she watched as his eyes opened and clashed with hers. Desire and lust collided and then Aaron sprang into action, like a big panther who'd been Tasered. He grabbed her sweatshirt, yanked it off her body and dragged first one nipple, then the other into his mouth, his hands diving between her legs. Then his fingers stilled and he pulled his head back to look at her.

"You're so wet."

Kasey nodded. Giving him pleasure made her hot. "I want you."

Aaron growled and pushed her yoga pants and panties down her hips, commanding her to step out of them. She was just free of her clothing when he lodged an arm around her butt and walked her over to the bed, laying her down. In one smooth movement, he wrapped his hands around the backs of her knees, lifted her up and pulled her open. Without waiting, he plunged inside her, filling every inch of her. There was no finesse or skill, this was pure sex, unleashed and as powerful as a summer storm. Kasey gripped his hips and held on as he whipped her higher and then higher still.

"I can't wait much longer. Dammit, Kase, come!"

His command flew over her skin and Kasey felt the explosion, the cosmic bang from deep inside her. She felt Aaron's thrust, felt his crown against her womb, and then he froze before she felt the jerks deep inside her that told her he'd followed her into the blast.

Kasey held him while he shuddered, his face in her neck, his big body covering hers. Taking shallow breaths, she wrapped her limbs around him, holding on as his shudders turned to sobs and she felt his tears on her skin, rolling over her collarbone.

She cradled him, wishing he knew that this place, in her arms, was where he belonged but knowing that Aaron, being Aaron, didn't believe he belonged anywhere.

Nine

Despite having his back to the door, Aaron knew when Kasey stepped into the downstairs living area of his house. It had something to do with the way the air stirred, energy moved. He'd never been so in tune with anybody, emotionally or physically, as he was with Kasey Monroe, and her holding that much power scared the crap out of him.

Aaron felt her eyes on him, reproachful and sad. Since their arrival back in Royal this morning, he'd barely spoken to her except to ask her to contact Will Sanders and Cole Sullivan and tell them to meet him at the house. Kasey had faxed Deputy Jen's reports to Cole and a few minutes after he and Will arrived at his house, Cole had confirmed his worst fears: Jason's DNA matched that of the sample taken from the body recovered from the plane crash, it was his ashes in the urn at Megan's house. Jason was dead.

The rest of the day had been equally hellish. Will fetched Megan and Savannah from Megan's house on the outskirts of town and, while Kasey distracted Savvie, Aaron had broken the news to his sister that their sibling was dead, probably by her husband's hand. He'd braced himself for Megan's grief, had expected her to throw herself onto his chest, but she'd, instinctively, turned to Will for comfort, folding herself into his big arms and quietly weeping against his chest. Aaron felt both upset and relieved that she'd turned to Will; upset because he knew that he wanted to be the one to comfort his only sibling, relieved because he didn't know if he could.

Aaron turned around and saw that Kasey was now standing by the kitchen counter, and he resisted the urge to cross the room to her, to step into her arms. Instead, he looked into her eyes and saw her need to comfort him, to hold him tight. A part of him wanted her to do exactly that but he knew that if he allowed her in, if he leaned on her, he might never let her go again.

And he knew that he had to let her go.

He was in crisis mode, had been since he'd first heard about Jason's disappearance and that he needed to care for Savannah. He'd been scared and out of his depth and, not used to feeling either of those things, he'd started to look to Kasey for support. It was natural but it was also stupid. Because, in a few months, when the rock on his chest had lifted a fraction and he had a little distance between his grief and, yeah, this clawing anger, he'd revert back to being the man who preferred to be on his own, to walk his own path, alone.

It was better if they parted company now, before she started to think there was a chance that she might move in here permanently, that she would be the mom Savvie so desperately needed. And, Jesus, this hurt to admit but…yeah. She needed to go before he fell in love with her and found himself unwilling—or unable—to let her go. As he well knew, losing people hurt, dammit! Whether it was by death or breakup, having someone be an integral part of your life and then not having them in that space sliced and diced one's heart. It was smarter to not put yourself in that position in the first place.

"Savannah's finally asleep," Kasey said, her voice sounding infinitely sad. "Megan is just washing her face, she'll be down in a minute or two. Will is in your office, making calls."

Aaron turned to face her, pushing his hands into the front pockets of his jeans. After telling Megan about Jason, and after her first bout of tears had passed, he'd asked her to help him tell Savannah. It was Megan's suggestion for Kasey to be with them and it had been the right decision. Like he'd anticipated, Savvie had turned to Kasey for comfort. The little girl had wrapped her arms and legs around Kasey's body and sobbed and then sobbed some more. Megan had tried to take her but Savvie had refused to relinquish her hold on Kasey. It was Kasey who'd taken her up to bed, who'd coaxed her into sleep.

He was mourning his brother, angry over what had happened to him, and all the while he was fighting his feelings for Kasey. Which meant Savvie's attachment to her temporary nanny was becoming a problem. The little girl was going to be heartbroken, again, when Kasey left. He should put some distance between them and Kasey, and the best way to do that would be to tell her to leave, to send her back to live in her own house. But it was too soon, Aaron thought, way too soon. He couldn't do that to the distraught little girl.

And let's be honest here, you want her to leave because it would be easier for you. You're not acting in Savannah's best interests, Phillips.

Telling Savvie that her best friend was leaving her life just after hearing that her father was dead would be a double blow to Savvie...

God, he couldn't do it. He *wouldn't* do that. He wasn't that much of a selfish prick.

Savannah's needs came first and he'd just have to find a way to live with Kasey. Maybe in a month or two, when Savannah felt settled, he could start easing Kasey out of their lives. Would that work or would Savvie be even more attached to Kasey than she was now? Would he?

God, he just wished someone would tell him what the hell to do!

Megan walked into the room, Will on her heels. It was obvious that Megs had been sobbing, her eyes were fire-engine red and swollen. Her face was pale and her hair was a mess but, Aaron noticed, his sister was still a beautiful woman. Aaron started to cross the room to pull her into his arms, to give her the comfort she so obviously deserved, but Will cut him off, yanking Megan into his arms, holding the back of her head to his chest. His eyes met Aaron's over Megan's head and Aaron read the back-off command in his eyes.

And, judging by the way Megan's hands gripped Will's hips, she wanted comfort from Will and not from him. Fair enough, Aaron conceded, ignoring the bitter taste in his mouth. For the last decade, up until Jason's disappearance, he and Megan hadn't been much more than casual acquaintances, so he wouldn't be the one she turned to in a crisis. But it hurt, dammit. He was her older brother, she and Savannah were the only family he had left.

Aaron felt Kasey's hand on his back—he hadn't seen her move across the room—and it felt natural to lift his arm to pull her closer, to absorb some of her strength. However, he came to his senses at the last moment and stepped away from her, lifting his shoulder to make her drop her hand. He couldn't rely on her. Not now, not ever.

Aaron saw the flash of hurt on Kasey's face and felt his stomach knot. He had to start the process of distancing himself at some point and he might as well start now. After all, he couldn't possibly feel more crap than he currently did.

Or maybe he could, who the hell knew?

Cole, thank God, broke the tense silence by clearing his throat. He'd forgotten that the private investigator was still there. "Shall we all sit down?"

Aaron nodded, perched on the arm of the closest chair and noticed that Kasey took the seat as far away from him as possible. Anger-tinged hurt flashed in her whiskey-colored eyes as she crossed those long legs. She also looked wiped, Aaron thought, noticing the dark circles around her eyes.

"As you know, Jason's DNA matches the body found in that crashed plane," Cole said, and Aaron appreciated his calm demeanor. "The DNA is also a match to the ashes in the urn you received, Megan, the ashes we originally thought were Will's. If you aren't convinced, we can send the samples to another lab for a second round of testing. Is that what you want to do?"

Aaron looked at Megan, who shook her head. Jason was dead. No amount of DNA testing would change that. "There's no point, Cole. The dispatcher saw the body, she commented on his resemblance to me. It's definitely him." Megan, tucked into Will's side, released a small sob. Aaron stared at the floor. After a minute of listening to Megan cry, Aaron looked at Cole, then Will. "There's something I haven't told you. I haven't had the time. I don't know if it's important but it's definitely odd."

He looked at Kasey and she gave him a small nod, encouraging him to continue. Cole's eyes locked in on him and Will, his arms still around Megan, cocked his head. "Kasey and I were at the Glass House on Saturday night—God, is today only Monday? It seems like a month ago." Feeling bone-tired and emotionally shattered, he looked at Kasey, wishing he could touch her because the world was starting to slide out from under his feet again.

"Glass House. Dinner..." Cole prompted him.

Right. He looked directly at Will. "You sent me a text earlier that evening saying that you and Cole were at the ranch, discussing the case. I replied back that I might try to meet you later, but it was a crazy evening."

Between Kasey looking like a sex goddess and him trying not to act like an idiot around Mark Ward, he'd tucked his worry about Jason away for a few hours.

Aaron felt the wave of guilt and grief swamp him but he kicked his way to the surface, knowing this was important. "I was looking around the restaurant and a group in the far corner stood up and your back was to me."

Will lifted his eyebrows. "Me?"

Yeah, this was where it got tricky. "Or somebody I thought was you. Shorter hair, wearing glasses, but your height and weight. I wanted to excuse myself to have a word with you, then I remembered that you said you were at the ranch. It had been a long and confusing day and I thought I was seeing things."

Cole and Will exchanged a long glance before Will shook his head. "I never left the ranch that night."

"So, someone was at the Glass House on Saturday evening who looked like you, Will," Cole said, folding his big hands and widening his stance. "Let's connect the dots…" Cole took a sip of whiskey and placed his glass on the stone mantel. "Abigail Stewart saw Jason and Fake Will, aka Rich Lowell, fighting and it's common knowledge that Rich and Jason boarded that plane together. Nobody filed a flight plan. Shortly thereafter, a small-town sheriff gets a report of the crash and, instead of launching a proper search and rescue, retrieves a victim from the crash. One victim, not two. What happened to the other person on the flight?"

Will started to speak but Cole held up his hand to stop him from interrupting. "Let's go for the most logical explanation, which is that passenger number one incapacitated passenger number two, exited the plane—probably by parachute—and the plane, flying on autopilot, crashed into the mountain. Then Sheriff Orson goes against all protocol to retrieve the body. doesn't order an autopsy, falsely identifies the body and arranges for it to be cremated. His deputy, following protocol, reported the crash to the aviation authorities and that's how I stumbled on the call sign."

Will nodded. "Sounds to me like the sheriff was paid off."

Well, yeah. Aaron had already worked that out for himself.

"Rich, acting as Will, was the last person to see Jason, the last person with him. If Jason became suspicious of who he was and what he was doing, then Jason would've had to be—" Cole hesitated "—dispersed of. It makes sense that Rich set up Jason to die in that crash and he walked away. Rich, with Sheriff Orson's help, pretended that Jason was still alive, sent the urn and the letter, supposedly from Jason, to Megan announcing his own—Will's—death, allowing him a new start."

"But if Aaron's eyes can be trusted, and I believe they can, Rich is still on the loose and back in Royal."

But why? Aaron wondered. Why come back to the place where everyone thinks you are dead? It made no sense.

Megan leaned away from Will, furious. "Rich is back in Royal? I swear to God, I'm going to kill him!"

"Settle down, honey," Will murmured, pulling her back to his side. "You are staying out of this."

"We have to play it cool, Megan." Cole sent her a sympathetic look. "If Rich is back, there has to be a damn good reason why he'd risk his neck to show his face here. Something has pulled him back here, because he's taking a hell of a risk. That tells me that he has unfinished business, and that makes him dangerous."

Aaron frowned. "What would be important enough to him to pull him back here?"

"Knowing Rich, money or revenge," Will said, anger in his eyes.

"Could it be connected to the money he stole from the Texas Cattleman's Club?" Aaron asked.

"Maybe. But revenge can't be ruled out, it's probably a combination of both," Will replied. "So, who is potentially in danger? Me. Megan…and you, as well, Aaron, if he thinks that Jason confided in you about his suspicions."

"I agree that you and Megan could be in danger,

me not so much," Aaron replied. "But we shouldn't take any chances. Megan can move in here, with me."

"Megan will move into the main house at the Ace in the Hole," Will said, his tone suggesting nobody should argue with him. "I'll protect her there."

Aaron saw that Megan was about to argue and lifted his hands. "You two work it out and let me know."

He looked at Megan. "We need to think about making a death announcement, holding a funeral for Jay."

Cole held up his hand. "Until we know where Rich is and what he's planning, I strongly suggest that the news of Jason's death stays in this room."

"Our brother is dead, Cole!" Megan cried.

Cole looked sympathetic but still tough. "He'll still be dead next week and the week after that, honey. I know it's hard but keeping his death a secret will make it easier to catch Rich, we don't want him bolting. You want him caught, don't you, Megs?"

"Damn straight I do," Megan retorted before nodding. "Okay, we'll keep it a secret, for now."

Aaron nodded his agreement and turned to Will.

"You need to take this to the FBI." He felt a burst of impatience at Will's suddenly blank face. "I know you are working with the FBI and other law enforcement, Sanders. You, too, Cole."

"I can talk to them until I explode, but it's all supposition, Aaron," Cole said, his voice calm. "And it all hinges on your sighting of Rich, which you admit was very short and fleeting. Add to the fact that you have been under enormous stress and that you are grieving, the assumption will be that you are clutching at straws."

"I saw him!" Aaron shouted and, out of the corner of his eye, saw Kasey jump a foot high in her chair.

Cole didn't back down. "I'm not arguing with you. I'm just telling you that your word isn't proof, that your story would be easily dismissed. We need more."

"Our brother slammed into a mountain!" Aaron roared, losing his grip on his temper.

"I need solid proof that Rich was involved, Aaron," Cole insisted.

His calm demeanor infuriated Aaron. Feeling like he needed to punch something, or someone, he shot to his feet and headed to the sliding doors. He needed air. He needed the silence of the night. He needed to walk to the end of his property and to scream, maybe to cry.

What he didn't need was to be in this room, listening to this crap.

He felt Kasey following him and as he stepped out onto the patio he whirled around to glare at her. "Will you goddamn give me some space? You are Savannah's nanny, not mine! Leave me the hell alone!"

Kasey nodded once, folded her arms against her chest and planted her feet. She blinked back her tears, nodded and spun around, holding her head high as she walked past his sister and the men. Aaron, feeling like a total dick and regretting his temper, tracked her movements until she disappeared into the hallway and, in the pin-drop quiet, he heard her feet on the wooden stairs. Without looking back at the rest of his guests, Aaron whistled for the dogs and disappeared into the night.

"I've had enough."

Kasey looked down at the plate Savannah pushed away and saw that she'd eaten a healthy portion of her breakfast, not as much as she'd like, but enough. She wasn't going to nag Savannah into eating more on her first day back at school after hearing about her father's death.

It had been hard enough for Kasey to coax her out of bed, coax her into dressing, into eating something. Savannah hadn't wanted to go back to school but after talking to the school principal and school counselor, Kasey realized that it was best for Savannah to be with her friends, to have a few hours of distraction. School was where Savannah needed to be, so it was Kasey who had made that happen.

She made everything happen, at the moment, Kasey thought as Savannah went to brush her teeth. For the last week she'd answered calls from both Aaron's friends and business associates, asking why Aaron wasn't taking their calls or answering his emails. She interacted with Savannah, keeping the little girl busy and entertained. Savannah was clingy and, naturally, weepy and on the other end of that scale, Aaron was cold, distant and noncommunicative.

She was everything to Savannah and nothing to Aaron.

Something had to give and soon... Savvie wasn't the only one who'd had enough.

Kasey checked her watch and noticed that it was nearly time for Megan to collect the little girl for school. Megan had been wonderful over this past week, picking Savannah up most afternoons and taking her back to Megan's house. Will hadn't succeeded at convincing Megan to move to his ranch for protection from psycho Rich—at least not yet. Kasey knew Will might not let go of the argument until Megan relented.

The doorbell rang and Kasey hurried into the hallway to greet Megan. As she opened the door, Savannah ran down the stairs, looking a little excited.

"Anything interesting happening at school today, Savvie?" Kasey asked as they walked out of the front door and down the stairs to Megan's vehicle.

"Puppet show," Savvie answered, sliding her hand into Kasey's and resting her head against her biceps. Savvie looked up and her eyes filled with tears. "Is it okay if I laugh a little today, Kasey? Would Daddy mind?"

Blinking back tears of her own, Kasey bent so that her eyes were level with Savannah's. "Savvie, of course he wouldn't mind if you laughed."

Out of the corner of her eye, Kasey saw Megan leave her car and then her hand was on Savvie's shoulder. Kasey flicked a quick glance at Megan and saw her concerned expression. "Savvie? Why would you think that it's not okay to laugh?"

Savannah stared down at her pink sneakers. "Yesterday, I was watching cartoons and I laughed. Uncle Aaron heard me and he slammed his glass down, said a bad word and stormed out of the room. He looked mad."

Kasey heard but ignored Megan's low hiss of angry surprise. Placing both her hands on Savannah's shoulder, she pulled in a deep breath and met the child's amazing green eyes. Like Aaron's eyes, they were chock-full of grief and guilt. "Honey, I know your daddy would be fine with you laughing. He loved you more than anything in the world and he only ever wanted you to be happy."

"But Uncle Aaron was mad because I laughed," Savvie protested. "And he is sad and mad because Daddy's dead, so I should be like that, too."

A classic example of kids watching what adults do, taking their cues from them on how to cope.

And Uncle Aaron was going to have six layers of skin stripped off him for being an insensitive ass, Kasey silently told her. "I'm sure he was mad about something else and that it had nothing to do with you."

Kasey pulled Savannah in for a hug, resting her cheek on Savannah's head. "If you don't hurry now, sweetie, you're going to be late for school. And while you're driving maybe Meg can tell you some funny stories about when she and your daddy were kids and the silly things they did."

Savannah's eyes lit up. "Daddy was silly?"

"I think he was. And remember, Sav, that you can talk to Meg and me and Aaron about your dad being dead, but no one else, okay?"

"'Cause you're trying to catch the bad man?" Savvie asked as Kasey opened the door for Savannah to climb into the car.

Kasey watched as Megan pulled away, catching a glimpse of Savannah leaning forward in her seat to hear Megan's stories about Jason. The child needed to talk about her dad, she needed to express her grief and keep his memory alive. Megan would try to do that but Savannah needed Aaron to step up to the plate, as well.

The silent, surly beast was ripping the little girl in two and it stopped, right now. Kasey hurried through the house, almost running by the time she hit the patio. Standing at the end of the pool, she waited for Aaron to stop, but instead of acknowledging her presence, he just turned and headed in the opposite direction.

Oh hell, no. He wasn't going to brush her off. She could cope with Aaron giving her the cold and silent treatment but she was damned if she'd let him hurt his niece, the child of her heart. When Aaron ignored her a second time, Kasey looked around, her eyes landing on a pile of fashion dolls Savannah had left on the outdoor table. Picking up a handful she resumed her place at the edge of the pool and hurled a doll at Aaron. It bounced off his shoulder and, because she could, she let fly with another three.

Two missed but the third hit him in the head. Aaron dropped his feet and, standing shoulder-deep in the water, glared at her.

"What the hell was that for?"

"You knew I was trying to get your attention and I don't like being ignored!" Kasey let the last doll fly and Aaron jerked his head out of the way at the very last minute. Pity, Kasey thought.

"What the hell is wrong with you?" Aaron yelled, swimming to the side of the pool and easily hoisting himself out. Kasey felt heat rush to between her legs as her eyes skimmed over those hard muscles and acres of masculine skin. God, she missed him. In her bed and out. She missed being in his arms, being the recipient of those half smiles, the desire in his eyes.

"Well?" Aaron asked, standing in front of her, scowling.

"Well, what?"

Aaron pointed to the plastic dolls floating face-down in the pool. "Want to tell me why you brained me with those?"

Oh, right. Kasey whirled around, picked his towel up from the lounger and tossed it at his chest. She couldn't think properly with all that skin on display, skin and muscles she wanted to glide her hands over, that surly mouth she wanted to kiss more than she wanted to breathe. But she wanted more than the great sex, she wanted his fears, his laughter, his grief. She wanted to comfort him and love him…she wanted to be a part of his life.

But this wasn't about her, it was about Savannah. Looking past him, Kasey stared at the pool.

"I can cope with your surly attitude and the silent treatment, Aaron. You haven't spoken more than a sentence to me since the day we flew back from Durango City." Kasey saw that he was about to object but she silenced his response with a fierce scowl. "You don't owe me a damn thing, but your silent and broody attitude is affecting your niece and *that* I won't tolerate!"

"You won't *tolerate*?" Aaron lifted a supercilious, I-am-the-boss eyebrow. "Last time I checked, you were working for me, Monroe."

"Oh, get over yourself!" Kasey retorted. "I am the only one interacting with Savvie, the one who holds her at night, who dries her tears, who damn well talks to her, so don't you dare pull that I-am-the-boss crap with me! She's scared to laugh at a puppet show today because she thinks that her dad wouldn't like it."

Aaron, admittedly, looked genuinely horrified at that. "Why would she think that?"

"Oh, it might be because you slammed down a glass, cursed and then stormed out of the room when she laughed at something she saw on TV."

Aaron shook his head. "I don't remember doing that and if I did, I'm sure I wasn't angry because she was laughing!"

"It doesn't matter whether you did or didn't, she thinks that. She thinks that she has to be mad and sad because you are. She's hurting, Aaron, and she sees you hurting and she thinks that she has to act like you do." Kasey rubbed her hands up and down her face before looking at Aaron again, suddenly feeling utterly vulnerable. "It's been five days but that little girl needs you, she needs to know that she'll be okay, that

you'll be okay, that she isn't going to be living with a surly, broody man for the rest of her life."

Kasey pulled in a deep breath, thought, *What the hell?* and plowed on. "She misses you, Aaron, and I do, too. I miss being with you, touching you, talking to you. I miss my friend and my lover."

Aaron pushed his wet hair off his face and Kasey saw the misery in his hard eyes, the brief tremble in his bottom lip before he firmed his lips. "Yeah, I've been meaning to talk to you about that."

Oh, God, that didn't sound good. "But first, Savannah." He rubbed the back of his neck and nodded. "I'll try and do better with her. Be more open, more interactive."

"She needs your affection, Aaron. She also needs to talk about Jason."

Aaron immediately shook his head. "I don't think I can. It's too hard."

Kasey slapped her hand on his chest and pushed. "This isn't about what you need, Aaron, this is about Savannah. She's the child, you're the adult, and her needs come first."

Aaron sent her a hot look, like he was prepared to argue, but then stepped back, putting space between them so that she had to drop her hand. He stared down at the pool and eventually nodded. "Okay, I hear you. I'll do better with Savannah."

Kasey lifted her eyebrows, knowing her will-you-do-better-with-me question was all over her face. Aaron cursed and shook his head. "I'm not going there, Kasey, not with you."

"Going where?" she asked, feeling the chambers of her heart starting to separate.

"Wherever your fantasies are taking you, there's not going to be a happy-ever-after for you and me. Not the way you envision. There's not going to be a you and me and Savvie living here with two ridiculous dogs, being the perfect family."

Kasey just stared at him, trying to hold her heart together, unable to respond.

"Savvie needs you right now, but I don't, not the way you want me to. I need you to help me with my business, to help Savannah through this horrible period of grief, but when our lives find a new type of normal, Savannah and I will live here on our own and you'll go back to being my virtual secretary."

Really? It seemed that Aaron had this all planned out, knew exactly what the future held and that he expected her to toe the line. The hell she would. She was damned if she'd fall into line just because some man said so.

"I love you, Aaron, more than you'll ever know and at the moment, because you're being an ass, probably more than you deserve."

She saw the horror on his face and rolled her eyes. "Oh, relax, I'm not asking you to love me back, my love isn't conditional. But what I won't accept is you tossing out commands about my life and what I do with it. You're not my boss, Aaron, from the moment I stepped into this house I've been working with you, not for you." Kasey suddenly knew exactly what to do. "I'll take Savannah to school and then I'll go back

to my house and work from there, relieving you of my company. When *I* think Savannah is emotionally stronger—and it will be my decision because you are emotionally constipated—I will start spending nights at my cottage, extending the time apart until she feels like she can do without me on a day-to-day basis. I will stay in touch with her and God help you if you try to stop me, Phillips. That's my girl in there and I will fight you, billionaire bucks or not!

"When Savannah is stronger, I'll resign and find something else to do. I didn't need Dale and I sure as hell don't need you. Yes, I love you and I'd love a family, a man who can treat me with the respect I deserve, who can love me through thick and thin. I'm a good bet, Aaron, and you're the idiot for not being brave enough to see that!"

Kasey registered the shock on his face but she was too angry to enjoy it. "I'm going inside before I do, or say, something I really regret. Or before I brain you with a chair."

Because the urge to do exactly that was strong, Kasey thought it best to walk away.

Ten

Aaron rubbed his towel over his head and watched Kasey's beautiful, slender frame cross the entertainment area and disappear into the house. Dropping to sit on a lounger, he reluctantly admitted that he'd screwed up and he'd done an awesome job at it.

Kasey loved him. Or she thought that she did. For an instant he'd been desperate to believe her, to allow himself to hope but then, just in time, he remembered that he'd heard it all before and declarations of love were easy to make. Despite what Kasey said, love was conditional, nobody loved without wanting something in return.

Despite longing for what she offered, the family he once thought he wanted, he was right to walk away.

And, although he'd been lost in grief and anger

and guilt, Kasey was right to pull his head out of his ass. He had left her to do the heavy lifting with Savannah, partly because his niece was so much more responsive to Kasey than she was him and, yeah, because it was easier to let Kasey deal with Savvie's emotions. He was having a hard enough time dealing with his own.

But Savannah was, ultimately, his responsibility and not Kasey's, and he'd never shirked his responsibilities in his life...until now. Aaron, seeing Jason's disappointed face in his mind's eyes, rubbed the moisture off his face, not all of which was pool water, and made a promise to his brother to do better. Jay was relying on him, wherever the hell he was, to make sure that Savvie had the type of childhood, life, Jason would've given her. And that meant that she needed a father and not the shadow man he'd been these past few days.

I'll try, Jay. It might take me a while, but I'll get there. Be patient with me, okay? I've got to learn to be a dad.

He could, and would, learn to be the best dad he could be for Savannah and to honor his brother's memory. But that was as far as he was prepared to go. He meant what he'd said to Kasey, as soon as he got a handle on being a dad, and to some extent, a mom, Kasey would need to move out. They had to go back to normality.

Whatever normality was.

He wanted to protect himself, of course he did, but he needed to protect Kasey, as well. He couldn't give her what she wanted, what she needed. Oh, he had the big house and he'd acquired a cute kid she adored through tragic circumstances, and they had this insanely hot chemistry, but that didn't a future make.

Kasey would never settle for the little he could give her. He was a solitary man, an independent guy, someone who didn't need the reassurances and comfort love brought. He didn't trust easily—no, he didn't trust at all. As she'd pointed out, Kasey, nearly a year after working for him, still didn't know the identity of his core group of investors. She worked closely with him yet he couldn't fully trust her with his business. And if he couldn't trust her with that, how could he trust her, or anyone, with his heart? And it wasn't like he was overreacting or being melodramatic, he had good reason not to trust, to guard himself against the vagaries of life.

And his fear. Because, dammit, he was damned terrified that he would love and lose again.

He wouldn't be able to bear it if he fell in love with Kasey—as he was a hairbreadth away from doing— and he lost her. He'd survived his parents' death, had coped with Kate's betrayal and he would, sometime in the future, be able to cope with Jason's death.

There wasn't a shadow of doubt in his mind that loving and then losing Kasey, through death or a breakup or divorce, would destroy him. He'd gamble with tens of millions of dollars in the workplace and not break a sweat, but tasting the dream of Kasey at his side, raising Savvie as their own, possibly with more kids later on, living, laughing and loving her and then losing her and them and the dream...

Aaron felt his heart rate accelerate, noticed that his breathing was shallow.

No. He couldn't do it. He couldn't trust it to last and if—when!—it disintegrated, he'd fall apart too. He couldn't take that risk.

No, it was better for him, better for Savannah, in the long run, for them to part ways. Despite Kasey calling him an idiot, he still believed it was the smarter option.

It really was. It had to be.

It was a special type of hell to finally realize what you really wanted and know that you were never going to have it. Kasey lifted her coffee cup to her lips, barely registering that the liquid was cold. Although it was only lunchtime, storm clouds were building up outside, casting a strange green light over the neglected garden outside her cottage in Royal.

After Aaron's hard, cold, speech, she'd made good on her promise to put some distance between the two of them. Every morning she dropped Savvie off at school and instead of heading back to the office she shared with Aaron, she drove to her cottage, where she and Aaron communicated virtually.

Kasey picked Savvie up from school and ferried her to and from her after-school activities. Back at "the Shack," she ate supper with the Phillipses, trading as little conversation with Aaron as possible, put

Savvie to bed and retreated to spend the long night in Aaron's guest suite.

Rinse and repeat.

Kasey didn't know how much longer she could operate within the confines of their own Cold War. Being around Aaron and only talking to him via email and the occasional video call was more difficult than she imagined. They'd lost the easy way of communicating they'd enjoyed before she'd moved into his home and every conversation was short, stilted and underlined with sadness and regret. Well, it was from her side. She had no idea how Aaron was feeling because he hid his feelings behind his inscrutable mask.

Kasey thought that she knew heartbreak, that she'd experienced the pain of failed relationships, but nothing compared to loving and losing Aaron. Dale's cheating and Michelle's betrayal still hurt but it was now an oozing scratch compared to the open-heart surgery she was currently experiencing.

She wanted Aaron, ideally as her life partner—she wasn't brave enough to dream about being his wife—but she'd settle for being his friend. Unfortunately, she wasn't even that anymore, she was just a woman he'd slept with during an awful period of his life, who'd helped him out during a jam and whom he now wanted to shove firmly back into a take-out-at-work-only box.

A part of Kasey wanted to rail at him, scream at him for being so dense—didn't he see how good they could be together?—but another part of her sympathized with his fear of being hurt. He'd endured more pain than one man should in his lifetime and she couldn't blame him for running from anything, or anyone, who might cause him more.

The hell of it was that she wouldn't. She realized how rare it was to find someone as brutally honest as Aaron, a man who was a curious combination of sensitive but strong, and loyal to a fault. She felt totally secure with Aaron; with his mile-wide streak of integrity she knew that he would never cheat on her, that when he gave his word he would never renege on it.

But he'd never given her his word. Or anything else, and the sooner she accepted that irrefutable fact, the sooner she could start rebuilding her life.

Kasey stretched and, seeing how dark it was outside, flicked on her desk lamp. The wind rattled the windowpanes and thunder rumbled in the distance. She hoped the late summer storm would blow away her misery but knew that it might take a couple of summers of storms to feel marginally human again.

Melodramatic much, Monroe? Damn, this being in love—properly in love, grown up in love—wasn't any fun at all.

Her computer buzzed with an incoming call and Kasey's heart flipped when she saw that Aaron was calling. Stupid heart, being so excited to see him, even if it was by a computer screen.

Kasey touched her keyboard and Aaron's beautiful, much loved face filled her screen. He was in his office, dressed in a pale green T-shirt that matched his eyes. The scruff on his jaw was thicker than normal and worry deepened the creases around his eyes.

"There's a storm coming in," Aaron told her.

Kasey placed her forearms on her desk. "Yeah, I noticed that."

"They are predicting lashing rain and the possibility of hailstones the size of tennis balls," he stated. "Your house might get nailed."

Since there was nothing she could do, Kasey just shrugged.

"Savannah is safe at school, but I think you should come back here," Aaron commanded.

Kasey shook her head. "I'm not getting into my car now to run from a storm, Aaron. I'll be fine."

"Kase—"

"Don't!" she snapped. "Don't pretend you are worried about me, you're just worried that something might happen to the nanny and executive assistant you profess to need so much."

"I do need you!" Aaron shouted, looking angry. And worried.

"Pity that you don't need me the way that I want you to need me," Kasey said. The sound of her doorbell chiming reached her over the rising wind and drumrolls of thunder. "I've got to go, someone is at the door."

"Kase! Just get in your car and come home."

"Conversation's over." Kasey shook her head and pushed her chair back, wondering if he'd noticed how miserable she was. God, she couldn't do this much longer. The doorbell pealed again and she muttered a curse as she headed into her tiny hall to yank open her front door.

Wet and shivering, Dale stood on her porch. Her first thought was that he was going to catch a cold—he always did—quickly followed by the wonderful realization that her ex being sick wasn't her problem anymore.

Lightning crackled and Kasey pulled Dale into her hall. "What are you doing here?"

"I've been trying to talk to you for weeks," he told her, pushing his hair off his wet forehead. "I drove up so that you and I could have a conversation."

Kasey thought about pushing him out the door, then decided that maybe it would be better to let him get whatever he had to say off his chest so that they could move the hell on. She was so over him.

Wanting to make this quick, Kasey didn't invite him to sit. She just stood in front of her desk and lifted her eyebrows.

"Speak."

Dale looked down at the floor and shuffled his feet. "I know that you won't believe me since I did what I did, but I love you, I always have. I need you to know that."

Kasey snorted and then a sudden thought occurred to her that rocked her world. *No. Freaking. Way.* "Are you trying to tell me that you want me back?"

The hope on his face gave her her answer. Kasey shoved her hands into her hair and laughed, the sound filled with genuine amusement.

"What's so funny?" Dale demanded.

"You are." The lights flickered as the storm threw a temper tantrum outside. "Dale, you don't know what love is and, honestly, neither did I. Love is honesty, it's reliability, it's responsibility. Love is steady, calm, it's inextricably linked with integrity. I now know what love is and it isn't with you and the life I left behind. It's here, in Royal. Love, for me, is Aaron and Savannah."

Dale lifted his lip in a sneer. "Well, I suppose it doesn't hurt that the guy is loaded."

"I would live in a tin shack with him if he asked me to!" Kasey slapped both her hands against his chest and shoved him, making Dale stumble back. "He doesn't want me, you moron! But that's the thing about love, you can't just turn it off and on. I will always love him because love doesn't fade when it's inconvenient, when there's something better to do!"

She swallowed a lump in her throat, forcing herself to go on. "He's in the process of moving me out of his life and my heart is breaking, but worse than that, I know his heart is breaking and there's nothing I wouldn't do to take his pain away! If he had to ask me the smallest thing, or the biggest, today, tomorrow, ten years from now, I would move heaven and earth to give it to him because there's nothing—*nothing!*— I wouldn't do for him. He, and that little girl, are my world. Just because I am not his, doesn't change a damn thing because love isn't selfish, dammit!"

Dale shrugged. "I'll give you some more time, it'll blow over with him."

"It won't and you should consider us completely done, Dale."

His face hardened as her words sunk in. Then his

expression changed, becoming harder and meaner. "You mean that, don't you?"

"You have no idea how much."

Dale's lips tipped up in a nasty smile. "Then there's something you should know…" Kasey didn't nibble on that bait, but he carried on regardless. "It wasn't just once."

The wind had kicked up and hard rain started to lash the windows, and Kasey heard the sharp ping of hail on her roof. Dammit, the storm had arrived.

A crack of lightning lit up the room and highlighted the spiteful look on Dale's face. "Michelle and I didn't sleep together just once, it wasn't just one drunken encounter. We had an affair while you and I dated, again shortly after we were engaged. It carried on, on and off, the entire time we were married."

Kasey stared at him, waiting for the wave of hurt, the jolt of pain. When none came, she looked inside herself and checked. Nope, nothing.

Well, huh.

"Nothing to say?"

Kasey took a moment to find the correct response to adequately convey how little she cared. Dale and Michelle were firmly in her past and she intended to leave them both there. She winced at the expensive sound of glass shattering in her back bedroom courtesy of a big hailstone. Dammit! A crack of lightning sizzled through the air, quickly followed by angry thunder.

"Kasey?"

"I deserve better than this. I'm tired of being tired

and I'm tired of giving you and her my energy. I'm done," Kasey stated, as calm as the storm outside was vicious. "I don't care anymore. About you. Or her. Or what you did together."

Somewhere close, a bolt of lightning made contact with the earth, the exclamation point at the end of her sentence and, as if to drive her point home, she and Dale were plunged into darkness.

Great, Kasey thought, being caught in a storm with her less-than-useless ex was exactly what she *didn't* need!

Aaron cursed as the picture of Kasey's nice ass and the sound of their voices faded from his screen. A loss of power was the most logical explanation for the abrupt lost connection and he knew that area of Royal was prone to electrical failures in big storms.

But dammit...

Aaron found himself staring at his monitor, not seeing the icons on his desktop or the ticker tape of stock prices rolling across the bottom of his screen.

She loved him? She'd always be there for him? Today, tomorrow, in ten years' time? She'd do anything for him? Sure, Kasey had told her that she loved him but he hadn't believed her, hadn't realized the depths of her feelings. It hadn't been an off-the-cuff statement, she'd meant every word. More than he realized.

Tin shack? Nothing she wouldn't do for him? Unconditionally? Her words bounced in and out of his brain. She loved him?

Holy crap.

Kasey loved him. Loved him loved him. Properly. Genuinely. Forever.

Aaron felt his breath catch in his throat, felt his heart expand. That amazing, wonderful, giving, sexy woman loved him? He felt like he'd been dropped to the floor by a right hook from a world heavyweight boxer.

He needed to hear her say those words to his face again, to fall into that space where he felt...God, safe. Kasey made him feel safe. He trusted her.

Aaron rubbed his hands over his face, trying to get his heart to restart and his breathing to slow down. He trusted her, he could finally admit that out loud. He probably always, subconsciously, had. He couldn't imagine handing over Savannah's care to anyone he didn't trust, allowing someone he had doubts about into his business, into his bed, his mind...his *heart.*

He'd tried hard to fight it, to fight her, but it was no use—he trusted her with everything he had and the final barrier to love, to being in love, falling in love, was removed. He didn't have an excuse anymore to be alone, to stay alone.

To raise Savannah alone.

This wasn't about Savannah, he realized, and if he found the courage to lay his heart on the line, he had to make it very clear to Kasey that he did need her, and not because he needed help raising Savannah. He needed her because he could be utterly authentic with her, brutally honest. She valued honesty and loyalty as much as he did.

Today, tomorrow, in ten years' time—Kasey made a pledge and he knew that she'd stick to it. And the fact she didn't need him to love her to make that promise floored him. She loved him unconditionally, utterly...*honestly.*

Unconditional love...not love based on his money or earning capacity, on whether he had a college degree. She loved him for who he was and not what he did.

God.

Realizing that the storm had tapered off, Aaron jumped to his feet, determined to get to her, to drop his heart at her feet. He snatched up his keys and when he reached the door, he stopped, halted by a powerful thought. He was running to Kasey because she loved him, she was prepared to give him what he needed, to fill the holes in his life. But could he give her what she needed? This had to be a two-way street...

What did she need?

A husband, a family, security...emotional safety. He'd never cheat on her, they enjoyed each other's company and would have a rocking sex life. Children? They already had one, they could cope with a couple more. So far, so good. Could he love her?

Aaron looked deep inside himself and suddenly realized that it wasn't a question of could, he did. He wasn't sure when he'd started to love her but he thought it was pretty soon after she moved into this house. Did the *when* matter? Wasn't the *how* more important?

He'd move mountains for her, given the chance. If that wasn't something she required of him, then he vowed to make damn sure that she knew, every day of her life, that she was the center of his world. That he'd love every day, every moment, they had together, grateful for the gift she was.

Aaron slapped the frame of the door, switched off the light in his office and headed for the stairs, determined to start this new chapter in his life as soon as he could.

The storm had been fast and furious and over within a half hour. In that short time, it managed to turn her lawn into a lake, punch a hole through her spare bedroom window and uproot the small live oak next to her driveway.

Kasey stood on her driveway and ignored Dale as he crossed the road to climb into the driver's seat of his car. He was leaving her life for the final time and she couldn't be happier about it. Right now she had bigger problems than Dale—and Michelle—to deal with, she had a little girl to collect from school and a house and a yard to clean up.

Kasey heard the low purr of a familiar engine and sighed as she noticed Aaron's familiar SUV turning the corner onto her street. Ah, crap. Now she also had her grumpy, bossy boss to handle.

Really? Couldn't she catch a break? Not willing to rumble with Aaron, she pulled her car keys out of the back pocket of her jeans and pressed the remote control to open her garage door. Hurrying into the small garage, she thought that, if she was really, really lucky, she could be in her car and halfway down her driveway before Aaron pulled up. She'd yell something about collecting Savvie and she'd manage to avoid him for another couple of hours.

Kasey had started to back down her driveway when she saw Aaron in her rearview mirror, pulling… God, what was he pulling across her driveway? Slamming on the brakes, Kasey yanked on the handbrake and flew out of the car. She stopped a little way down her driveway and spent a minute watching Aaron as he pulled a heavy branch across the driveway, directly behind her car.

"What the hell are you doing?" Kasey demanded.

Aaron didn't look at her and Kasey's eyes bounced from his face to the bulging muscles in his arms. "Pulling this damn branch across your driveway."

"I see that. Want to explain why or have you just lost your mind?"

That half smile she'd missed so much touched Aaron's mouth. "To stop you running away from me."

He could've just parked his SUV behind hers to stop her from driving away… Okay, none of this was making a lick of sense. "I do have to collect Savannah at three."

"Depending on how the next fifteen minutes goes, I'll either move the branch or ask Megan to collect Savannah," Aaron said. He looked toward the road where Dale was still sitting in his car, looking at them.

"Why is moron-head still here?" Aaron demanded, glaring at Dale.

"I don't know." Kasey narrowed her eyes at him. "Not that him visiting me has anything to do with you."

Aaron tipped his head. "Really? Actually, I think it has a lot to do with me."

Tired, sad, confused…Kasey wished he would just go. Spending a little time with Dale made her realize how unsuited he was for her and how well she and Aaron gelled. And knowing that hurt because Aaron didn't want her in his life…

Kasey pushed her hair off her face and looked up at the gray sky. "Just go, Aaron," she begged. "I'm tired and I have the insurance company to call, damage to sort out."

"I'll help you do all that…later," Aaron told her, stepping up to her. "Right now we are going inside and we're going to have a chat."

She couldn't bear to hear the repeat of his "we'll be okay on our own" speech. Of course they would be okay but if they were together they could be a million times stronger and better. Kasey shook her head and lifted her chin. "Just go home, Aaron."

"Okay, then, if you're going to be like that." He placed his hands on her hips, hoisted her over his shoulder in one easy, fluid move, and Kasey found herself dangling down his back. From her upside-down view of the world, she saw Dale's car driving off.

Forgetting about him, she tried to smack Aaron on the ass. "Put me down, you jerk! What the hell!"

"We need to talk," Aaron told her, walking through her front door and kicking the door closed with his foot. He pulled her down and Kasey found herself sliding along his body, his very hard, very "hey, I'm excited to see you" body.

Kasey looked up and her eyes collided with his, amber clashing with pure green. Kasey opened her mouth to say…something but before she could speak the words she was still forming, Aaron's mouth covered hers in a kiss that was as tender as it was sexy, as hot as it was loving. Beneath the shimmer of lust, the layer of desire that always flooded them whenever they touched, she felt something deeper, wiser, infinite in his kiss.

Something she'd never experienced before.

Pulling back, unsure whether her imagination was running wild, Kasey yanked her mouth from his and lifted her fingers to her lips, feeling bewildered.

"What the hell was that?" she murmured.

"That was me, kissing you, the way I intend to kiss you for the rest of our lives."

The rest of their…*what?*

Confused, Kasey allowed Aaron to tug her over to her desk and watched as he picked up a permanent marker, yanked the top off with his teeth and, turning her wrist over, scrawled a few random letters and numbers on her arm.

"What is going on with you?" Kasey demanded, her eyes bouncing from her arm to his face.

"Master code. To my client files, my bank accounts, pretty much everything. With that code you have all the access I can give you to every aspect of my life without compromising my clients' privacy."

"Okay." Kasey frowned. "Why?"

Aaron bent his knees so that his eyes were level with hers. "Because I trust you, Kase. With everything I have, everything I love, I trust you."

Uh… Kasey knew that she was repeating herself but…

What. The. Hell?

She stared at Aaron, wide-eyed and slack-mouthed. "Have you lost your mind?" she asked.

Aaron clasped her face in his big, warm hands, his eyes drilling into her. "Did you mean what you said to your ex? That you loved me, would always love me and that your love wasn't conditional on whether I loved you?"

Kasey frowned. That was the way she felt but she'd never said those exact words to his face. "Why would you think that?"

Aaron looked impatient and jerked his head at her computer screen. "You answered the door but didn't kill the call. I was still there."

Kasey frowned at him. "You listened to my conversation with Dale? That was rude, Phillips!"

"I don't give a damn!" Aaron snapped back. "I want to know if it's true."

Kasey tossed her hair. "What part?" she demanded, stalling for time, conscious of heat filling her face.

"All of it. Specifically, the part about you loving me unconditionally."

Crap. Kasey sighed and looked down at the floor.

She'd hoped to keep her pride, hoped to have kept that salient little piece of information to herself.

Kasey felt Aaron lift her chin. "Kase, look at me. Did you mean what you said?"

Kasey nodded. "Yes." She stared at his pale green T-shirt. "Sorry," she added, shrugging.

Aaron pulled her to him and wrapped his arms around her, his big body enveloping hers. "Don't be sorry, Kase. Please don't be sorry for loving me."

"I'm more sorry that you can't love me back." Kasey spoke the words into his broad chest, into the fabric of his T-shirt.

From above her Kasey heard the sound of a soft laugh. "Well, now, that's not completely true."

Kasey pulled back and scowled up at him. "What is that supposed to mean? You love the sex, you love the way I love Savannah, my cooking? What?"

Aaron looked contemplative. "The sex is earth-shattering, I do love the fact that you love Savannah and your cooking is meh at best."

Kasey rolled her eyes before trying to remove herself from his strong grip. "Let me go, Aaron."

"Not in a million years," Aaron told her. Placing his one hand on her lower back, he pushed his fingers into her hair, holding the back of her head so that she had no choice but to look up. "No more games or wordplay, Kase. Here it is, as forthright and as honest as I can be."

Kasey's eyes widened as she lost the ability to speak.

"I'm utterly, crazy, wildly, in love with you and I

only realized it when I heard you tell your ex what I mean to you. I refuse to apologize for my eavesdropping because that conversation changed my world, it opened up my eyes and freakin' ripped me apart, in the best possible way."

Kasey blinked once, then again, but Aaron was still gazing at her with love and adoration in his eyes. "Uh—"

"And I'm not telling you I love you because I need a mom for Savannah or because you are a kick-ass assistant or because I need you in either capacity. I'm telling you I love you because you are... Everything. You are my everything."

Kasey felt tears burning her eyes as she lifted her hand to hold Aaron's much loved face. "Air..."

"Yeah." Aaron closed his eyes briefly, opened them and looked bashful. "I don't have the words, Kase, but I trust you, with everything. With Savvie, with my secrets, with my clients—all of them." He tapped the writing on her wrist. "But most of all, I trust you with my battered, mangled heart."

Kasey, knowing Aaron's issues with trust, got how big those words were, how massive his declaration. If he had told her he loved her but still couldn't trust her, then his love wouldn't mean much; with Aaron love and trust were inextricably intertwined.

Aaron lifted her hand and kissed her knuckles. "Don't go, Kase. Stay with me. Be mine."

Kasey nodded once and the tears she'd been trying to blink away rolled down her cheeks. She wound her arms around Aaron's neck and buried her face in his shoulder, her own shaking with love and relief.

Aaron rubbed her back before releasing her, his thumbs stroking the tears off her cheeks. "Kasey, honey? I love you. You, amazingly, love me. Isn't this supposed to be a good thing?"

Kasey nodded. "I just didn't know how I was going to say goodbye to you and Savvie."

Aaron pulled her back into him and it felt natural to boost herself up, to wrap her legs around his waist, confident that he would support her, in any way she needed, for the rest of her life. "Warning—I'm never letting you go."

"I don't want you to," Kasey told him, her smile on his lips. "I love you so much, Air."

Aaron's face softened as love and adoration danced in his eyes, across his face. "I love you, too, baby." Holding her, he lifted one arm to look at his watch. "I really want to tell Savvie that we are going to be a family but we have a little time." He pretended to think. "I wonder what we can do until then?"

Kasey grinned impishly at him. "Move the branch blocking my driveway? Board up my broken window? Call the insurance company?"

Still carrying her, Aaron started to walk down the hallway to her bedroom, his smile pure sexiness. "Yeah…screw that."

Epilogue

Late the next afternoon, after spending the day in Royal, Kasey walked into Aaron's office to find him on the phone. She smiled when she saw Savannah lying on the floor next to Aaron's desk, coloring, the puppies sitting at her feet.

"Scar, how are you? How's California?" Aaron asked, leaning back in his chair and speaking via speakerphone. His eyes softened as he looked at her and Kasey's heart filled with love. Everything that mattered to her was in this room at this exact time.

Aaron held out his hand to her and she crossed the room.

"All good, Aaron. I'm so sorry to hear about Jason. How's the peanut?"

"I'm okay, Auntie Scarlett," Savannah piped up.

"Sad but okay. When are you and baby Carl coming back to Royal? You need to meet my New-find-me puppies."

"Soon, honey. I miss my animals and my friends and my family. I have some news, Aaron. Luke and I were married a few days ago, on the beach, but we're going to settle down in Royal."

Aaron grinned as he pulled Kasey onto his knee, lifting his head in a silent demand to be kissed. Kasey brushed her lips across his before curling up against his chest. He smiled as he congratulated Scarlett and Kasey heard his happiness for his friend in his voice. Who was she again? As if reading her mind, Aaron picked up his pen and jotted Scarlett McKittrick, Veterinarian, and Paradise Ranch across the piece of paper in front of him. Ah.

Aaron's hand moved under Kasey's dress and up her thigh. She shivered and he smiled at her, heat and promise in his eyes.

In the background, Kasey heard the sound of a male voice calling Scarlett's name. "I've got to run. When I'm back, bring the new additions to the family to the clinic so that I can check them over and give them their shots. And bring your new girl, too," Scarlett said.

"There's a deal," Aaron said, smiling as he disconnected the call.

Kasey wound her arm around Aaron's neck and was about to give him a proper, missed-you-like-hell kiss when she saw Savvie scrambling to her feet. Savannah rolled her eyes and placed her hand over

Kanga's and then Roo's eyes. "Ugh, more kissing. Let's go, boys."

Kasey blew her a kiss and Savvie smiled before running out of the room, the dogs on her heels. Instead of kissing Kasey, Aaron picked her up and perched her on the edge of his desk. "Sit there for a minute so that we can talk without me getting distracted."

Kasey smiled. They got distracted a lot lately and, currently, not a hell of a lot of work was happening at AP Investments. "Okay."

Aaron stood and placed his hands on his hips. "How did your meeting go with Michelle?"

Kasey shrugged. "It's done. She begged a little, cried a little, tried to lie her way out of it, but I think she's finally accepted that she's no longer a part of my life."

Aaron looked relieved and then concerned. "Are you okay with that?"

Kasey shrugged. It still hurt but she was okay. "I'm making new friends so I will be."

Aaron smiled. "The book club crew. Those women are dangerous."

"But so much fun," Kasey replied.

Aaron's wonderfully green eyes turned serious. "When you walked in just now, I realized that my life started when you walked into it." He bit his bottom lip and shook his head. "But as happy as I am, I have to ask you, again, if you truly know what you are taking on. Savvie and I are a package deal, Kase. Are you ready for that? For her? For me?" Aaron stared down at his feet, his expression a little tortured. "I wouldn't blame you if you wanted some time to think about this."

Did he really think she'd walk when he needed her the most? Kasey placed her hand on his arm, waited until he looked at her. "I love you and I'm not going anywhere, Aaron."

He looked relieved but still a little stubborn. "If you're here because you're worried about me jumping into investigating Jason's death, I told you I wouldn't. I know that I have to leave it to Cole and Will to manage. It pisses me off but my priority is Savvie. And you."

Kasey knew he wanted to, that he was as frustrated as hell standing on the sidelines. "Good to know, but I'm still not going anywhere."

Aaron pushed an agitated hand through his hair. "I need you to be sure, Kase. We're talking marriage, making us a family…it's all serious stuff."

So serious and *everything* she wanted. Kasey stood and placed her hands on his hips, tipping her head back to look up into his face. "Air, I can't wait for the future…our future. You and me, together. We are a team, we're stronger together than we are apart. As for Savvie, I love her, Air. She's the child of my heart. Even if we have a dozen more, she'll always be my first."

Aaron rested his forehead on hers, tension seeping out of his body.

Kasey kissed him once, then again. "Are we good?"

"Yeah. I love you," Aaron murmured, his smile

as warm as sunshine against her lips. Aaron's arms pulled her closer and his mouth brushed hers, full of love and desire. Kasey felt her heart settle and sigh, she was home and all was good with her world.

Then, from outside the door, Kasey heard Savannah admonishing one, or both, puppies. "Kasey's going to be so mad... Why do you guys have to eat her stuff? She's not going to let you be flower dogs when they get married if you don't learn to behave!"

"No dogs at the wedding," Kasey told Aaron.

Aaron used one finger to push a strand of hair off her cheek. His voice was pure tenderness when he spoke. "You say that but we both know that you will walk up the aisle to me with a little girl and two crazy dogs at your side."

He was right and, frankly, Kasey couldn't imagine it happening any other way.

* * * * *

Don't miss a single installment of the
TEXAS CATTLEMAN'S CLUB:
THE IMPOSTOR.

*Will the scandal of the century lead to love
for these rich ranchers?*

*THE RANCHER'S BABY
by* New York Times *bestselling author Maisey Yates*

*RICH RANCHER'S REDEMPTION
by* USA TODAY *bestselling author Maureen Child*

*A CONVENIENT TEXAS WEDDING
by Sheri WhiteFeather*

*EXPECTING A SCANDAL
by Joanne Rock*

*REUNITED...WITH BABY
by* USA TODAY *bestselling author Sara Orwig*

*THE NANNY PROPOSAL
by Joss Wood*

*SECRET TWINS FOR THE TEXAN
by Karen Booth*

*LONE STAR SECRETS
by Cat Schield*

***

*If you're on Twitter, tell us what you think of
Harlequin Desire! #harlequindesire*